BETTER
the feel good place

Lincolnshire
COUNTY COUNCIL
Working for a better future

Lincolnshire Libraries
This book should be returned on or before the due date.

Bourne

27.9.23

D1352289

By Stephen Leather

05357782

ALSO BY STEPHEN LEATHER

Pay Off, The Fireman, Hungry Ghost, The Chinaman, The Vets, The Long Shot, The Birthday Girl, The Double Tap, The Solitary Man, The Tunnel Rats, The Bombmaker, The Stretch, Tango One, The Eyewitness, Penalties, Takedown, The Shout, The Bag Carrier, Plausible Deniability, Last Man Standing, Rogue Warrior, The Runner, Breakout, The Hunting, Desperate Measures, Standing Alone

Spider Shepherd thrillers:
Hard Landing, Soft Target, Cold Kill, Hot Blood, Dead Men, Live Fire, Rough Justice, Fair Game, False Friends, True Colours, White Lies, Black Ops, Dark Forces, Light Touch, Tall Order, Short Range, Slow Burn, Fast Track

Spider Shepherd: SAS thrillers:
The Sandpit, Moving Targets, Drop Zone, Russian Roulette

Jack Nightingale supernatural thrillers:
Nightfall, Midnight, Nightmare, Nightshade, Lastnight, San Francisco Night, New York Night, Tennessee Night, New Orleans Night

CHAPTER 1

The lightning cast shadows of the trees outside onto Lucy's bedroom curtains and she hugged her teddy bear and counted off the seconds until she heard the rumble of thunder in the distance. 'Six seconds,' she whispered to her bear. 'That means it's just over a mile away.' She pressed her cheek against the bear and flinched at another flash of lightning. 'One elephant, two elephants, three elephants, four elephants, five...' The bedroom windows shook as a clap of thunder rang out, the loudest yet. 'That means it's getting closer,' she said. She hugged the bear tighter but it didn't make her feel any better. She slipped from under the duvet and padded over to the door, hoping that she could get to it before the lightning flashed again. She pulled the door open and hurried towards her mother's bedroom. The door was ajar and she pushed it open and stepped inside. 'Mum, I'm frightened, can I sleep with you?' she whispered. There was no reply. 'Mum, I'm scared,' said Lucy. She took a step towards the bed but stopped when a flash of lightning illuminated the room for a fraction of a second. The bed was empty. Then the darkness was back and she was counting again. 'One elephant, two elephants.....'

She clasped the bear to her chest and went back to the hallway. The bathroom was next to her mum's bedroom. The door was open and the light was off. A loud thunderclap split the air when she reached four elephants, so powerful that it made her stomach turn over. But the sound that came after the thunder was a thousand times more scary - she heard her mother begging. 'Please, please don't.'

Lucy walked slowly across the carpet to the bannisters where she could look down into the sitting room. Sometimes when her mum sent her to bed, Lucy would creep out and sit at the bannisters and watch television as her mum sat on the sofa. It had always felt like a safe place, but not tonight.

Lucy gasped as another flash of lightning illuminated her mother lying on the sofa, a big man looming over her. The man was dressed

1

all in black and had a wool cap on his head but she could see his face clearly. Her mum was lying on the sofa, her hands over her face.

The room was plunged into darkness and Lucy started counting again but almost immediately there was another flash. The man had tied a scarf around her mother's throat and was pulling it tight. For a fraction of a second Lucy locked eyes with her mother and then it was dark again and she was just a shadow. The man moved over her and put his knee on her chest and when the lightning flashed again, Lucy couldn't see her mother's face.

Lucy dropped her bear and backed away from the bannisters, her hands over her mouth.

A clap of thunder shook the light fitting above Lucy's head. She looked around frantically. She didn't know who the man was or how he could have got into the house. Her mum was always careful to make sure all the doors and windows were locked, ever since dad had left them to live with his secretary three years earlier.

Was the man alone? What if there were more men in the house. She jumped as something banged down in the sitting room. It sounded as if the coffee table had been tipped over. Lucy kept her back to the wall as she moved slowly along the hallway to her bedroom.

There was a flash of lightning and she saw a giant shadow cast across the bottom of the stairs. She turned and ran towards her bedroom. She hurried inside and closed the door. She went to her wardrobe. It was one of her favourite places when she played hide and seek with her friends. She opened the door. It was her favourite place but they always found her eventually. She closed the mirrored door just as another flash of lightning showed her reflection. Her blonde hair was in disarray, her skin was pallid and her eyes were wide and fearful. Then she was back in darkness.

Under the bed. She could hide under the bed. But wasn't that the first place anyone looked? She stood in the middle of the room, panting. She had a sudden urge to hug her bear but she had dropped him in the hall. She heard a squeak from the stairs but it was immediately blotted out by a long roll of thunder. She remembered something her father had said, before he'd left. He'd been talking to her about what to do if there was ever a fire. Keep low, he said. It was the smoke that killed you, not the flames. But if there was too much smoke, or the heat was too bad, she was lucky because she could escape through her window. The window overlooked a garage and it wasn't a big drop and her father had said that if she was ever in danger she could get out that way.

Lightning flashed and she hurried towards the window. It was raining and the drops were splattering against the glass. As she pushed the window up, water blew in, soaking her face. She climbed onto the window sill. Her father had told her the safest way to drop would be to hold the window sill and lower herself as far as possible before letting go. Her nightdress was already soaked and her hair dripping wet as she eased herself down. Just as she was about to lower her head below the sill there was a flash of lightning and she saw her bedroom door opening. She let go of the window sill and fell backwards, into the rain.

CHAPTER 2

Tommy O'Keefe banged his NHS walking stick on the floor. 'I need to go to the fucking toilet and I need to go now!' He glared around the room. 'I'm going to piss myself again!' There were fifteen people in the day room, but no one was paying him any attention. Mrs Kincaid was in her usual spot, a high-backed winged armchair by the door. She was counting on her fingers. No one knew for sure what she was counting, but that was what she did, hour after hour, day after day.

Three female residents were sitting on a plastic sofa facing a television set showing an Australian soap opera. Their combined age was just shy of two hundred and seventy and they had all been transferred from a home in Bradford which had been gutted by fire the previous month. All were in various stages of dementia and clearly had no idea where they were.

'For fuck's sake, why won't anybody help me?' shouted Tommy, and he banged his stick again.

Sitting at a table by the window were two men playing dominoes. Charlie Cooper was in his late-seventies, with silvery grey hair that was slicked back and he was peering at the dominoes through horn-rimmed spectacles. An old wooden walking stick was leaning against the wall next to him. His playing partner, Billy Warren, was about the same age but looked a fair bit older with pallid skin and watery eyes. Charlie was wearing a corduroy jacket over a plaid shirt and a wool tie. Billy was more casual, as usual, sporting a black polo neck sweater with the sleeves pulled up, and Levi jeans.

There were fifty-five dominoes in total, from double zero to double nine. When they had first started playing they had used a double six set but the games went too quickly and the one thing they had plenty of was time so they had switched to the larger set.

'We should get one of those clock things,' said Billy.

Charlie frowned. 'What clock things?'

'You know, those clock things they use in chess matches.'

Charlie looked up from his tiles. 'What the fuck are you talking about?'

'You've been staring at them for five fucking minutes.'

'I'm thinking.'

'For five fucking minutes?'

'Not about this,' said Charlie, waving his hand at the tiles on the table in front of them. He gestured at the room. 'About this.'

'What about this?'

'I fucking hate it here.'

Billy laughed. 'We all hate it here. But what can we do? I've written a shit review on TripAdvisor but it didn't make any difference.'

'I'm serious, if I don't get to the toilet now I'm going to piss myself!' shouted Tommy from the far side of the room.

Billy looked around. 'Where the fuck has Everton gone?'

'He was here five minutes ago.'

'Yeah, well he's not here now and Tommy sounds serious.'

'He's wearing diapers, isn't he?'

'He refuses to wear them. Anyway, he's not incompetent, he just needs help to go.'

'Incontinent,' said Charlie.

'What?'

'The word is incontinent. Incompetent is what you are.' He put down a tile. 'Your go.'

'Yeah, give me a minute,' said Billy. He put his hands on the table to help push himself up off the chair, and walked across the room to Tommy. He walked by Mrs Dean, who had recently celebrated her 90th birthday and who was convinced that Billy was her son, Jim.

'Jim!' she shouted.

'Hi mum, I'm busy right now,' said Billy, giving her a friendly wave. Billy knew from experience that correcting Mrs Dean always ended badly, with the woman getting tearful and agitated. It was better just to go along with her.

'Okay,' she said, and went back to staring into space. She was dribbling from the corner of her mouth and her lips were dry and flaking. Mrs Dean's son had died five years earlier but even when he was alive he rarely visited his mother. Now that he was dead, she had no one. She was one of the longest-serving residents. She had survived several bouts of flu and shrugged off the coronavirus as if it had been a head cold, but dementia had taken its toll and she spent most of her days in a mindless haze, sitting at one end of a plastic sofa, her hands in her lap. The only time she ever perked up was when she saw Billy.

Billy went over to Tommy and he looked down at him. 'What's the problem, you old fart?' he asked.

'I need a piss!' shouted Tommy.

Billy grinned and held out a hand. 'Come on, I'll take you,' he said.

Tommy grunted and reached out to grab Billy's arm with gnarled fingers. The nails bit into Billy's flesh like talons as Tommy hauled himself out of his chair, using his stick to help. When he finally managed to get to his feet he swayed back and forth, breathing heavily. Billy waited until Tommy had steadied himself, then walked him slowly across the room. As they passed Mrs Dean, she waved excitedly. 'Hello Jim!'

'Hello mum,' said Billy.

'Mad as a hatter,' muttered Tommy.

'Her or me?' asked Billy.

'Both of you.'

Billy walked Tommy to the door, then took him along the corridor to the toilets. The door to the staff room was shut. Billy had half a mind to knock to see if there was anyone on duty but it was clear that Tommy was running out of time. They reached the toilet and luckily it was unoccupied. Billy pulled the cord to switch on the light and helped

Tommy inside. There was a lemon-scented air-freshener on a glass shelf above the sink but it did nothing to cover the smell.

There were chrome safety parts around the toilet and an alarm cord with a red handle which summoned help when pulled. The sink taps had extensions on so that they could be operated with elbows and there was a pedal bin labelled BIO-HAZARDOUS MATERIAL There was no window but switching on the light also operated a fan which grated in the ceiling above their heads.

'Help me get my trousers down, will ya?' asked Tommy.

'You said you wanted a piss.'

'Yeah, well now I want a shit. Come on, don't fuck about.'

Billy sighed and undid Tommy's belt, then opened his trousers and pulled them down.

'And my underwear,' said Tommy.

'Tommy, you're not wearing underwear.'

'What?' barked Tommy.

'You're not wearing any fucking underwear. You're commando.'

'I wasn't a commando. I was in the guards. The Household Cavalry. That bastard nicked my medals.'

'Who?'

'You know who. The Irish tea leaf. Connolly. Fucking pinched my medals and then said I never had any.'

Tommy turned around, sat down heavily and immediately farted loudly. Billy backed away. 'Fucking hell, Tommy, give me a chance to get out, will you?'

'Where are you going? You know I can't wipe my own arse.'

'Tommy…' groaned Billy. He looked up and down the corridor but there were no caseworkers to be seen. He turned his back on Tommy, leaned against the walls and folded his arms. 'Go ahead,' he said wearily.

It took Tommy the best part of five minutes and a lot of moaning and grunting to evacuate his bowels, at which point he used his stick to get to his feet and shuffle around. 'I'm ready,' he said, and bent forward.

Billy sighed and tore a strip of toilet paper off the roll. He leaned behind Tommy and ran the wad of paper between his cheeks and wiped as best as he could. 'Get in there, it won't bite you,' said Tommy.

'I swear I will swing for you one day,' said Billy. The smell made him want to throw up but he gritted his teeth and did the best job he could of wiping Tommy's backside. It took three wads of toilet paper before Tommy was satisfied. Billy tried not to look at the soiled paper as he pressed the button to flush it away.

Tommy saw the look of disgust on Billy's face. 'Wait until you get to eighty,' he said.

Billy laughed. 'I'm eighty-four, Tommy.'

'Like fuck you are.'

'What can I say? Clean living.' Tommy wasn't able to pull up his own trousers so Billy did it for him, then fastened them and buckled his belt. He held Tommy's stick while he washed his hands using antiseptic soap from a dispenser on the glass shelf, then Billy washed his own. He'd just about got used to the smell as he opened the door and helped Tommy out into the corridor.

Tommy gripped Billy's arm with his left hand and steadied himself with his stick in his right as they walked slowly down the corridor towards the day room. The door to the staff room was ajar and Billy looked in as they went by. Three of the home's staff were drinking coffee. Jackie Connolly, a big bruiser of a man who had been a prison officer in Belfast, was sitting by the door. He had a military haircut and a neatly-trimmed moustache and his pale blue eyes hardened when he saw Billy. Sitting opposite him was Raja, an Indian guy in his thirties with Bollywood movie star looks and slicked-back glistening black hair, and Sally, a cheerful West Indian who was the longest-serving care-worker at the home.

Only Connolly saw Billy and Tommy and he kicked the door shut on them.

'Bastard,' muttered Billy under his breath.

'What?' asked Tommy.

'Nothing, Tommy, Come on, one step at a time.'

Billy helped Tommy down the corridor to the day room. As he reached the door, Everton Roberts came out of the dining room. Everton was a huge Jamaican with a shaved head and a broad smile that revealed two gold front teeth when he wasn't wearing a covid mask. He had a plastic apron over his blue overalls, bright yellow Marigold rubber gloves and was carrying a mop and bucket that smelled strongly of bleach. He frowned when he saw the two men. 'What's happening here?' he asked.

'Tommy needed the bathroom,' said Billy.

Everton put down the bucket and leaned the handle of the mop against the wall. 'You're not insured to help the residents like that, Billy,' he said. 'You should have called for help.'

'I did fucking call!' said Tommy. 'I shouted until I was blue in the face that I was about to shit myself and no one fucking came.'

'Language, Tommy,' said Billy. 'It's not Everton's fault.'

'Well whose fucking fault is it?' said Tommy. He began to cough and bent over double.

Everton rushed over to him and held his right arm. 'Are you okay, Tommy?' he asked.

Tommy took a deep breath to steady himself. 'I just need to sit down,' he said. He began to cough again.

Everton and Billy helped Tommy into the day room and over to his chair, then they carefully eased him down into it. Tommy's walking stick slipped from his bony fingers and Billy bent down to retrieve it.

Tommy grinned, showing a mouth devoid of teeth. 'Thanks, Billy. You're a diamond.' He took the stick and held the handle with both hands.

'Don't mention it,' said Billy. He grinned back. 'I'm serious. Don't mention it to anybody or I'll have to kill you.'

Tommy began to chuckle as Billy went back to the table by the window, where Charlie was still studying the dominoes in front of him.

'You love being the good samaritan, don't you?' said Charlie as Billy sat down.'

'He was going to shit himself.'

'How is that your problem?'

'Remember the last time he shat himself in his chair? The smell?'

'My sense of smell isn't what it was,' said Charlie. 'Not since that covid. My sense of taste never came back either, but considering the shit they feed us, that's no bad thing.'

Billy looked up from the table and shook his head. He sat back and folded his arms, and sighed. 'I know what you did,' he said.

Charlie looked up and smiled as if butter wouldn't melt. 'What?'

'You know what.'

'What?'

'You're cheating. You changed your tiles while I was away.'

Charlie's jaw dropped. 'How can you say something like that? I'm hurt.'

'You will be if you do it again, you cheating bastard.'

'Billy, on my mother's life....'

'Your dear old mum has been dead going on thirty years. Now look me in the eye and tell me you're not cheating.'

Charlie stared at Billy, his eyes narrowed. Billy stared back. They locked eyes for a good thirty seconds before Charlie burst into laughter and pushed his dominoes into the pile. 'You can't blame a guy for trying,' he said.

'What's the point of winning if you have to cheat?' asked Billy, pushing his own dominoes into the mix.

'Winning is the point,' said Charlie.

'But we're not even playing for money.'

'It's not about money,' said Charlie, with a grin. 'It's about winning.'

CHAPTER 3

Billy sighed and opened his eyes. Someone was crying, in one of the rooms along the corridor. It was a woman but that didn't narrow it down much because three quarters of the residents were female. Women lived longer than men, that was just a fact. And those extra years were at the end of life, obviously, and at the end of life there was a lot to cry about.

Billy sat up and took off his CPAP mask. He needed a continuous positive airway pressure tank to provide extra air as he slept, the result of a severe attack of the COVID-19 virus that had left his lungs and heart in bad shape. During the day his oxygen levels were generally fine but at night he tended to wake up gasping for breath unless he was attached to the tank.

He leaned across to his bedside table and opened the drawer. He took out a small clear plastic case containing two foam rubber earplugs. He rolled one of the plugs between his finger and thumb, then inserted it into his left ear canal. He repeated the process with his right ear. The plugs gradually expanded, cutting out the noise, but he still heard a man screaming off in the distance. Screams were as common in the home as crying. There were screams of pain, of rage, of frustration, screams for help and screams for medication. Sometimes the screams were answered but often they were ignored. Not long after Billy had arrived at the home, he had screamed at night, just the once. It had been a scream of frustration and he'd muffled it with his pillow. He had actually felt slightly better afterwards, but it was the first and last time. Screaming was as pointless as crying because, at the end of the day, nobody cared.

The earplugs continued to expand and eventually there was no sound, just the steady thump of his heartbeat. He re-attached the mask and lay down. Sleep never came easy. The mattress was hard and the two pillows were too soft for comfort, but Billy closed his eyes, sighed, and tried to fill his mind with happy thoughts.

CHAPTER 4

Charlie was already sitting at their usual table by the window when Billy walked into the dining room. There were only three window tables in the room. Charlie had already claimed ownership by the time Billy had moved into the home and had insisted on a half hour interview before agreeing to allow Billy to sit with him. Charlie always took the seat on the left, allowing him a view of the staff carpark and the entrance to the road.

The table was set for two and there were already two glasses of weak orange juice on the white plastic tablecloth. There were two triangles of toast in a stainless steel toast rack. Charlie was staring out of the window but he looked over as Billy sat down. 'Morning, squire.'

'Morning,' said Billy. He nodded at the toast rack. 'They both mine?' They were allowed one slice of bread each day at breakfast, cut in half. The crumbs and smear of jam on Charlie's side plate showed that he had already helped himself. Next to the toast rack was a tub of supermarket margarine and a jar of strawberry jam. The label on the jam jar was torn and faded from years of use, it was refilled every couple of days from a 5kg plastic container.

Charlie grinned, then reached over and took one of the two remaining triangles. 'The early bird gets the worm,' he said.

Billy shook his head. 'Help yourself, it's not much more than warmed up bread.'

Charlie added margarine and supermarket brand strawberry jam to his slice and took a bite. Everton came out of the kitchen carrying two plates and he brought them over to the table and put them down in front of them. 'Morning, Gents,' he said.

'Morning, Everton,' said Billy. He looked down at the plate and sighed at the scoop of watery scrambled eggs that had come from a packet, an orange frankfurter sausage and half a tomato.

Charlie picked up his knife and fork and tucked in as Everton walked away.

Billy looked around the dining room. There were two dozen tables in all, most of them seating four people though there were a few against the wall that were set up for two. There were three meals a day - breakfast between eight and eight thirty, lunch between twelve-thirty and one, and dinner at six. Not all the residents ate in the dining room, there were several who were so frail they took their meals in their rooms, served on the sort of trays they gave passengers in economy on budget airlines, complete with plastic cutlery. At least the meals in the dining room came on china plates with metal cutlery, but the quality of the food stayed the same.

'You want your sausage, squire?' asked Charlie.

'Knock yourself out,' said Billy.

Charlie leaned over and stabbed at Billy's sausage with his fork. 'I'm going to get some cereal,' said Billy. He stood up and walked over to a trestle table next to the kitchen. It was covered with plastic sheeting and there were three large Tupperware containers with Aldi cornflakes, instant porridge and muesli, and plastic jugs of milk, one of which was labelled SKMD. Billy poured cornflakes into a bowl and added a splash of regular milk. There was a blue plastic bowl of fruit at the other end of the table containing a few apples and two bananas. One of the bananas was speckled with brown but the other seemed in reasonable condition so Billy grabbed it.

As he walked back to his table, one of the women sitting on her own began to cry. She was holding a fork of scrambled eggs but her hand was shaking so much she couldn't get it to her mouth. Billy looked around but there were no care workers available to help. There were only three on duty - Everton was serving and Sally and Connolly were already attending to residents who weren't able to eat on their own.

Billy looked away as he went by her, embarrassed by her tears. He sat down opposite Charlie, then used his knife to cut the banana into pieces which he scattered over his cornflakes.

'You're not going to eat your eggs?' asked Charlie.

'I'm going to eat them, but I want my cornflakes first.'

The woman was still crying. Billy looked around. Sally was spoon-feeding Jimmy, a ninety-year-old Irishman who had once flown Jumbo Jets for British Airways. Jimmy could barely do anything for himself. He had to be washed and dressed in the morning, then fed, then wheeled into the day room where he would stare at the television with unseeing eyes.

Connolly was sitting opposite one of the female residents, Mrs Chalmers. Mrs Chalmers had dementia or Alzheimers, Billy wasn't sure which, and her attention span was so short that she couldn't feed herself. She had been a model in the sixties, and Everton had once shown Billy her portfolio. She had been a breathtaking beauty back in the day, and some of the photographs had been taken by the legendary David Bailey. In the photographs she was long-legged and had porcelain white skin and soft blonde hair cut short. She was heavier now and her hair was white and little more than a fuzzy halo around her liver-spotted skull, but she still had the most amazing green eyes.

Connolly was toying with her, holding out a spoonful of porridge and then moving it away each time she opened her toothless mouth.

'Leave it out, squire,' said Charlie. 'There's nothing you can do.'

Connolly held out the spoon and tapped Mrs Chalmers on the nose, leaving a streak of porridge on her skin. She tried to get her mouth to the spoon but Connolly moved it away again.

'He's a fucking monster,' said Billy.

'Yup, but he's a big bastard and if he gets on your case he'll make your life a misery and I might be collateral damage. Stop staring at him.'

Connolly tapped the spoon against the woman's chin. Even from across the room, Billy could see the tears welling up in her sorrowful green eyes.

'Bastard,' whispered Billy.

'Leave it alone,' said Charlie.

Connolly turned to look at Billy and for a second their eyes locked. Connolly's eyes narrowed, then a savage grin spread across his face. Billy looked away. Charlie was buttering the last slice of toast. He waved his knife at Billy. 'You've got to pick your battles,' he said. 'And you won't win against Connolly. The staff have the power in here, you know that. Prison rules.'

'We need to get the fuck out of here,' said Billy. He started to eat his cereal and banana.

Charlie took a bite of his toast and then dropped it onto his plate and piled scrambled egg on top of it.

'We need to get out of here,' said Billy again.

'I heard you the first time.' Charlie snorted. 'It's not as if we have a choice, squire.' He waved his knife around the room. Do you think anyone would choose to be here?

'I know,' said Billy. He picked up a stainless steel tea pot and poured some tea into his cup. He knew from experience that there was only one teabag in the pot and that it had to stretch to two cups. 'It's just…'. He left the sentence unfinished.

'I hear you,' said Charlie. 'But beggars can't be choosers.'

'Is that what we are, Charlie? Beggars?' He added a splash of milk to his tea. There was hardly any colour to it, or taste.

'As good as, squire,' said Charlie. He frowned as he looked over at the doorway. 'Hello, another lamb to the slaughter.'

Billy turned to see what he was looking at. A middle-aged woman with permed hair was pushing a wheelchair in which sat a grey-haired man wearing a dark blue polo shirt and brown trousers. She was wearing a plastic face shield and had the blue plastic shoe covers that they gave to what few visitors were allowed in. Next to them was the manager of the care home, Mrs Woodhouse. She had taken up the job after her predecessor had suffered a nervous breakdown in the wake of the coronavirus epidemic. Mrs Woodhouse was a no-nonsense married mother of two teenage girls. Her daughters occasionally turned up to

15

help at the home but it was clear from the constant look of disgust on their faces that Mrs Woodhouse used it as a punishment. Mrs Woodhouse was clearly giving her usual introductory talk, and the woman was nodding enthusiastically. Mrs Woodhouse had donned a face shield and was wearing latex gloves for the occasion. The man in the wheelchair was looking around but didn't seem happy at what he was seeing. Billy couldn't blame him. He'd had the same feeling of dread when he'd first set eyes on the Sunnyvale Nursing Home. Mrs Woodhouse could sugar coat it all she wanted but at the end of the day it was a place where people came to die. Billy shuddered. The man looked across at their table and made eye contact with Billy. Billy saw a flash of despair in the man's eyes before he looked away.

The woman patted the man on the shoulder as if offering her reassurance. The man turned and looked up at her and said something and she laughed and shook her head.

Mrs Woodhouse was pointing at the kitchen, probably explaining how often the residents were fed. The man looked at his watch as if he had somewhere to go.

'Seems okay,' said Charlie. 'Still has his wits about him by the look of it .'

'How old do you think he is?'

Charlie squinted over at the group. 'I dunno. Seventy-five?'

'Seventy-five? You think he's younger than me?'

'I dunno. Eighty? Eighty-five?'

'He's in a wheelchair.'

'That's nothing to do with age. We all end up in a wheelchair eventually. If we live long enough. Bloody hell, Billy, what crawled up your arse and died? I don't know how old he is and I don't care.'

The woman turned the wheelchair around and Mrs Woodhouse led them out of the dining room. Billy turned back to his cereal. 'I just wish I was somewhere else.'

'You and me both. But when you don't have two pennies to rub together, the council decides where we go. And we've been sent here.'

'And that's it. Fait accompli?'

'Fait a-fucking-ccompli it is, squire. Are you sure you're going to eat your eggs?'

'Take them,' said Billy. 'I've lost my appetite.'

CHAPTER 5

Charlie studied his dominoes and then looked at the tiles on the table over the top of his glasses. He sighed and wrinkled his nose. Billy sighed in frustration. 'What?' asked Charlie.

'Are you going to make a move, or not?'

'Of course I'm going to make a move. But I want to make the right move.'

'You're taking forever, Charlie.'

'Squire, time is the one thing we've both got plenty of.'

Billy groaned, folded his arms and leaned back in his chair. There was a game show on television, the sound up loud because many of the residents had hearing problems. The three old ladies from Bradford were sitting on a sofa staring at the screen. It was hard to tell if they were watching or not. Another resident was sitting in an armchair facing the television. Billy wasn't sure if her name was Emma or Amy, she seemed to answer to both. She spent most of her hours knitting though she didn't seem to be making anything in particular. Her current project appeared to be a scarf but it was already at least ten feet long and she seemed in no hurry to finish. The first section was red, then she had switched to yellow and then blue, and now she was using green wool.

Everton was kneeling down next to Tommy. Everton was chuckling and Billy figured Tommy was telling him one of his many off-colour jokes. Tommy could barely remember what he'd eaten for breakfast or where he'd left his slippers but he could reel off dozens of dirty jokes without pausing for breath.

A wheelchair appeared in the doorway. It was the man they'd seen earlier with the home manager. He'd changed into a red polo shirt and had a newspaper in his lap. The man looked around and nodded at Billy when they had eye contact. Billy nodded back. The man wheeled himself over to the television and parked next to the sofa. He said something to the three women sitting there but they ignored him. The man spoke again, louder this time. He was asking for the remote.

Billy chuckled. The remote had been confiscated during the coronavirus crisis and had never been returned. The only way to change channels or the sound was to use the controls on the set.

Charlie finally made his move. A double four. 'Are you kidding me?' said Billy. 'All that thinking to place a double?' He sighed and shook his head.

Charlie looked at him over the top of his glasses. 'It's the right choice, squire.'

'Of course it's the right choice. But why did it take you ten minutes to decide that?'

Charlie shrugged. 'I was considering my options.'

Billy put a tile down. A four to go against the double, with a nine showing.

Charlie nodded thoughtfully and stroked his chin. 'For fuck's sake,' Billy muttered. He looked over at the television. The man was leaning towards the nearest of the three ladies. He reached over and tugged at her sleeve. 'Are you watching this?' he shouted. She looked at him blankly, her mouth open. 'Never mind' said the man. He stood up and walked over to the television. Billy's eyes widened in surprise. 'What the fuck?' he said.

'Don't rush me,' said Charlie.

'Look at this,' said Billy. 'He can walk.'

Charlie looked up from the tiles and frowned as he saw the man lean over the television and fiddle with the controls. 'The Lord be praised,' said Charlie. 'It's a miracle.'

The man found the button to change channels and he began to flick through them. 'What's he playing at?' asked Billy.

'He's changing the channel,' said Charlie.

'I can see that you soft bugger,' said Billy. 'I mean what's he playing at with the chair?'

Horse racing appeared on the screen and the man straightened up. He watched for a few seconds, then went back to the chair and sat down.

'Well that's not something you see every day,' said Charlie. He shrugged carelessly and went back to studying his tiles.

CHAPTER 6

Billy came down the stairs just as Everton was helping Tommy towards the toilet. Everton was supporting Tommy by holding his left arm while Tommy had his stick in the right. 'You're one of the good guys, Everton,' said Tommy.

'Right back at you, Tommy,' said Everton. 'I wish all our guests were as respectful as you.'

'Did I ever tell you the one about the porn star, the vicar and the donkey?'

Everton chuckled. 'You did, Tommy, but you can tell me it again.'

Billy walked into the dining room, but stopped when he saw the man in the wheelchair parked at the table he and Charlie used. The man was reading a newspaper and sipping a glass of water. Billy went over and stood looking down at him, his hands on his hips. 'Hey, this is our table,' he said.

The man frowned up at him. 'Our table?'

'My table. Me and my pal Charlie eat here.'

The man's frown deepened. 'What, you have a reservation, like?'

'Not a reservation, no.'

'Because Raja said I could sit anywhere.' He waved his hand around the room. 'And this looked like a nice enough spot.'

'Yeah, you can sit anywhere. But not here. This is mine and Charlie's table.'

'What? Like a table for two?'

'Yeah. Exactly. Two. Me and Charlie.'

'But it's for four. It's a table for four.'

Billy sighed in exasperation. 'But it's where Charlie and I sit.'

The man smiled amiably. 'I'm not stopping you from sitting here, am I? It's a table for four. You, me and Charlie makes three. And if Nicole Kidman drops by, she can sit with us.'

Billy opened his mouth to reply but he couldn't think of anything to say so he ended up stammering 'B-b-b-b..'

Charlie came up behind him and put a hand on his shoulder. 'What's going on?'

'He's taken our table,' said Billy.

'Oh, so now I'm a thief, am I?' said the man.

'Look squire, this is where Billy and I sit. It's our spot. Our place.'

'Yeah, so he said. Are you two a couple?'

'What?' said Charlie.

'No,' said Billy.

'I mean, if you're gay and this is a non-heterosexual table then obviously Raja has made a mistake and I can't sit anywhere,' said the man. 'There's obviously been a misunderstanding. I'm not gay. Not that there's anything wrong with being gay, it's just that I've always liked women.'

'I like women,' said Billy, quickly.

'We're not gay,' said Charlie.

'So we're all good then,' said the man. He held out his hand to shake. 'Archie's the name.'

Charlie looked at the hand, then at Billy, then back to Archie. He transferred his stick to his left hand and shook with his right. 'Charlie.'

'Pleasure to meet you, Charlie,' said Archie. 'Looks to me like you're one of the few residents who's still got his wits about him.' He grinned and held out his hand to Billy. 'You too, mate.'

Billy shook his hand, still confused about what was happening.

'What's your name, mate?' asked Archie.

'Billy.'

'Pleased to meet you, Billy. Come on, sit down, no need to stand to attention.'

Billy and Charlie sat down. Charlie opened his mouth to say something but stopped when Sally arrived with three plates of food balanced precariously on a tray. She put them down in front of the three men. She was wearing a hair net and had a plastic face guard on. A plastic apron and latex gloves completed her outfit.

Archie frowned at his plate. 'Bloody hell,' he said.

'Language,' said Sally.

Archie looked up at her and smiled. 'Sorry, darling. What's your name, then?'

'Sally.'

'That's one of my favourite names, right there,' said Archie. 'Nice to meet you, Sally. I'm Archie. Can I have a steak?'

Sally frowned in confusion. 'A steak?'

'Exactly. Medium rare. With chips. And mushrooms.'

'Mushrooms?'

Archie nodded. 'Mushrooms. And a drop of pepper sauce would go down a treat.' He pushed his plate towards her. 'I can't eat this.'

'That's your dinner.'

Archie shrugged. 'I can't eat it. It's slop. I wouldn't feed this to a dog.'

Sally turned to walk away but Archie held up his hand. 'I want to make an official complaint,' he said.

Sally flashed him a tight smile. 'I'll get you a form.'

'A form?'

Sally sighed. 'If you want to make a complaint, you fill out a form.' She turned on her heels and walked away.

Archie looked over at Charlie, who had picked up his knife and fork. 'Is the food always this bad?'

'This is better than it usually is,' said Billy.

'Fuck me.'

'You get used to it,' said Charlie.

Archie poked at his food with his knife and fork. 'I don't think I'll ever get used to it. Are there even enough calories to keep us going? Maybe it's all part of the plan to save on pensions and health care. Kill us with covid and then starve anyone who survives the virus.'

Billy leaned towards Archie and lowered his voice. 'Can I ask you a question, Archie?'

'Sure. But not geography. I was always crap at geography.'

'You don't really need that wheelchair, do you?'

Archie narrowed his eyes. 'Why do you say that?'

Billy shrugged. 'Just guessing.'

Archie gestured at his wheelchair. 'I can't walk, mate. I lost the use of my legs.'

Charlie leaned towards him, his knife and fork pointing skywards. 'Yeah, but we saw you walk to the TV,' he said.

Archie grinned. 'Nah, not me, mate. Must have been one of them there optical illusions.'

Billy and Charlie looked at each other. They had both seen what they had seen. Archie laughed at their confusion. 'The look on your faces,' he said. 'It's a scam, innit.'

'A scam?' repeated Billy.

Archie looked around to make sure that they couldn't be overheard. Sally was serving a table on the other side of the room and Connolly was tormenting Mrs Chalmers at her table. 'The last place I was at was shit. The staff were thugs. I was on the third floor and there was no lift so I cracked on that I'd lost the use of my legs. They got sick of carrying me up and down the stairs and after a while they transferred me. I've got a ground floor room here.' He gestured at the plate in front of him. 'Mind you, if the food's always this bad, I might start walking again.'

Billy and Charlie laughed. Archie looked around for Sally, She had disappeared into the kitchen. 'She's not bringing back a form, is she?'

The two men laughed even harder. Charlie shook his head. 'No squire, she isn't.'

CHAPTER 7

Charlie and Billy were playing dominoes when Archie wheeled himself into the day room. Charlie waved him over. Archie grinned as he rolled up to the table. 'So this isn't a table for two, then ?' he said.

'Sorry about that,' said Charlie. 'We didn't know who you were. You just came out of the blue.'

'But I passed the audition?'

Charlie chuckled. 'You did.' He waved at the tiles on the table. 'Do you play?'

'I've been known to.'

'Wait until I've finished beating Billy and we'll have a three-hander.'

'He cheats,' said Billy.

'And he's a sore loser,' said Charlie.

Archie looked down at the tiles. 'So you use the double-nine set?'

'It makes for a longer game,' said Charlie. He went back to study his tiles, frowning thoughtfully.

'So why are you here, Archie?' asked Billy.

'Same reason as everyone else, mate. I got old.'

'No money?' asked Charlie, his eyes on his tiles.

'If I knew I was going to live this long, I'd have maybe saved a bit more,' said Archie. 'No money, no family, you go where the council puts you.'

'What about the woman who brought you in?' asked Charlie.

'My social worker. They called her when it went tits up at the old place. She wasn't happy. She'd thought she'd seen the last of me.'

26

'Have you got any family at all?' asked Charlie.

Archie shook his head. 'My wife passed away ten years ago. The Big C.'

Charlie looked up from the tiles. 'Cancer?'

'No, mate, she fell off the Isle of Man ferry and drowned.' He laughed at the look of confusion that flashed across Charlie's face. 'Of course it was cancer.'

Charlie chuckled. 'Nice one,' he said. 'What about kids?'

'Just a son. He married an Australian girl and lives in Brisbane. We were never close, truth be told. So really, no family to speak of. A few distant cousins maybe. What about you guys? Have you got family?'

Charlie smiled ruefully. 'If we had, we wouldn't be in this shit-hole, would we, squire?'

'Plenty of people here have families, Charlie,' said Billy. 'They just never visit.'

Charlie smiled thinly. 'This is God's waiting room. Just killing time, that's all we're doing. Waiting to shuffle off this mortal coil. Who said that?'

'You did, Charlie,' said Archie. 'Just then.'

Charlie chuckled and looked at Archie over the top of his glasses. 'I meant originally, you dipshit.'

Archie grinned. 'It was Shakespeare.'

'You sure?'

'Hamlet. It's in his "To be or not to be" speech.' Archie frowned as he tried to remember the quote. 'What dreams may come, when we have shuffled off this mortal coil, must give us pause.'

Charlie nodded, impressed. 'Fuck me, squire, nothing wrong with your memory. I can't even remember what I had for breakfast this morning.'

'It was shit,' said Billy.

27

'Fair enough,' said Charlie. 'But it's always shit.' He looked at Archie. 'So what did you do?'

'Work-wise, you mean?'

'Yeah.'

'I was a butcher. Had my own shop. Hell, I had four shops at one point. Then the supermarkets put me out of business.'

Billy nodded in agreement. 'It was the internet that did it for me. I was a publisher's rep. Used to travel the country selling books. Fucking supermarkets killed me when they started selling paperbacks. And Amazon. Don't get me started on Amazon.'

'What about you, Charlie?' asked Archie.

'I was a locksmith. Self-employed most of the time. Good steady work. Everyone needs security.'

'And you didn't save?' asked Archie.

'Two ex-wives and three kids between them,' said Charlie. 'The last divorce left me with two suitcases and a rented flat. That was what, fifteen years ago? The mistake I made was letting them divorce me. I should have just killed them.'

Archie laughed. 'I hear you,' he said.

CHAPTER 8

Archie opened his eyes and blinked at the ceiling in confusion until he remembered where he was. The home. A care home they called it, but there didn't seem to be much caring going on. He sat up and rubbed his hands over his face, then picked up his mobile phone. It was just after six and he'd set his alarm for seven but he didn't feel tired so he rolled out of bed and dropped to the floor. He did twenty brisk press-ups before rolling onto his back and doing twenty sit-ups. He showered and dressed, then picked up his cigarettes and lighter and sat down on his wheelchair. He rolled out of his room and along the corridor to a set of French doors that led onto a stone-flagged terrace overlooking the garden. He parked and lit a cigarette. Two seagulls were hovering overhead, looking down to see if he had anything to eat. When they realised he wasn't there to feed them they flew off. Archie blew smoke up at the clouds, then checked his phone. No missed calls, no messages. 'It's good to be popular,' he muttered to himself, then slipped his phone into his back pocket.

When he wheeled himself into the dining room, Charlie and Billy were already at their table. A place had been set for Archie but with no chair so that he could wheel himself into position. 'Good morning, gents,' he said. 'Sleep well?'

'Are you serious?' asked Billy.

'About what?'

'You didn't hear the crying?' Billy asked. 'And the screaming at three o'clock in the morning? It got so bad I had to put earplugs in.'

'I didn't hear a dicky bird,' said Archie. 'Maybe you should see if you can switch to the ground floor.' He grinned. 'Better class of inmate.'

Sally appeared with three plates on a tray and she put them down. Watery scrambled eggs, a spoonful of beans and grey boiled mushrooms. She flashed Archie a warning look as if daring him to say anything but he just smiled amiably and winked. As he turned to watch Sally walk away, he caught sight of Connolly, tapping a cereal-laden spoon against the chin of Mrs Chalmers. Tears were running down her cheeks. 'Why does nobody stop him?' asked Archie.

The two men looked over to see what he was talking about. Billy winced when he saw what Connolly was doing. 'He does worse than that,' said Billy.

'What do you mean?'

Mrs Chalmers opened her mouth wide but Connolly kept moving the spoon out of reach.

'He messes with the women,' said Charlie. 'In their rooms. And he steals. Don't leave anything of value in your room.'

'I don't have any valuables,' said Archie.

'I'm just saying. Be careful.'

'Somebody should report him.'

Billy grimaced. 'Fill in a form, you mean? Then what? He's a big bugger. He could snap your spine in half.'

'You need to keep an eye on your watch and that gold chain you're wearing,' said Charlie. 'He'll have them.'

Billy nodded in agreement. 'Yeah, he's like a fucking magpie, he'll grab anything shiny.'

Archie picked up his knife and fork and prodded his scrambled egg. 'This is from a packet, right?'

'It comes in a barrel, I think,' said Charlie. 'From China. Or Vietnam. It's actually not bad if you cover it with ketchup.'

Archie took a piece of toast and laughed out loud. 'What do they do to this?' He held the piece of toast aloft. 'Show it a photograph of the toaster?' He saw Raja at another table and waved him over. 'Raja, what's the story with this toast? Well I say toast. It's not even warmed up bread.'

Like Sally, Raja was in full PPE. He peered at the toast through his face shield and shrugged. 'The toaster's on the fritz, Archie. Sorry. I'm told there's a new one on order but who knows?'

'Can't you put it under the grill?'

'The chef's under pressure as it is.'

Archie laughed out loud. 'Chef? You're having a laugh.' He waved his hand at the plates on the table. 'No chef has been anywhere near this. Look, I'm not complaining about the reconstituted egg or the flavourless mushrooms or the Aldi beans, I just want a decent slice of toast to start off my day. Is that too much to ask?'

Raja put his hand on his heart and gave Archie a mock bow. 'Mr Jennings, you have my heartfelt apologies, I shall fetch a complaint form immediately.' He turned and hurried away.

Archie chuckled as he watched Raja rush off, then he turned back to the table.

'You know he's not coming back with a form?' said Charlie.

'Yeah, I gathered that,' said Archie.

'Go easy on Raja, he's one of the good guys,' said Billy.

'I was only messing with him,' said Archie. He dropped the piece of bread onto his side plate and reached for the tub of margarine. 'But how hard is it to make toast? It's not as if it's a secret recipe, is it?'

'I heard that councils spend just under £2.50 a day on food per resident,' said Charlie.

'Fuck me, that's the price of a cup of coffee in the real world.'

'Exactly,' said Charlie.

'We should complain,' said Archie.

'I'll get you a form,' said Billy, and the three men chuckled.

Archie reached for a stainless steel teapot and poured some tea into his cup. He frowned when he saw the colour of the liquid and lifted the lid. 'One teabag?' He said. 'For three of us?'

'It used to be for two,' said Charlie. 'But when you joined us, they just added more water.'

'Sorry about that, guys,' he said. 'I'll make it up to you.' He finished filling his cup with insipid tea and added a splash of milk.

'How will you do that, exactly?' asked Charlie, peering at him over the top of his glasses.

'I'll buy a box of teabags when we're out.'

'Out?' said Charlie. 'Who said anything about going out?'

'So what's your plan for the day?'

'Same as usual. Dominoes in the day room.'

'Fuck that for a game of soldiers,' said Archie. 'You can come for a drive with me.'

'A drive?' Billy repeated. 'What are you talking about?'

Archie spread jam over his toast and grinned. 'Trust me,' he said. He reached into his pocket and took out three strips of tablets and popped one tablet out of each.

Charlie grinned. 'Statins?' he said. 'We're all on them.' He pulled a pack of tablets from his shirt pocket. Billy did the same.

'Statins, a calcium blocker and Metformin to control my blood sugar,' said Archie. He popped the three tablets into his mouth and washed them down with tea,

'I was on Metformin but it gave me terrible gas,' said Charlie.

'It was disgusting,' agreed Billy. 'Couldn't take him anywhere.'

'They switched me to Canagliflozin and that works a treat,' said Charlie.

'What about the statins?' Billy asked Archie. 'I've had pains in my legs ever since I started taking them.'

'A bit, but nothing to worry about,' said Archie.

'I keep telling the doc I'd rather stop taking the statins but he says they reduce my chances of dying by twenty-five per cent,' said Billy.

'Which is bollocks because everyone dies eventually,' said Charlie, putting his tablets back into his pocket.

'Bloody hell, guys, give it a rest,' said Archie. 'All this doom and gloom is starting to get me down. I can see you two guys definitely need cheering up.'

CHAPTER 9

Billy and Charlie followed Archie out of the rear entrance of the home. Archie rolled down the wheelchair ramp and Billy and Charlie took the steps. Lined up against the wall were half a dozen mobile scooters in different styles and colours. Archie parked his wheelchair, stood up and stretched, and walked over to a black scooter with a chrome shopping basket on the front. He sat down and waved at the remaining scooters. 'Choose your rides, gentlemen.'

'We're not handicapped,' said Billy.

'Neither am I,' said Archie.

Billy laughed. 'Fair point.' He walked over to a red scooter and sat down. 'How do you work it?'

'There's an on-off switch. Forward to go forward, back to go back. Half the people driving these have got dementia so they have to make them idiot-proof.'

Charlie sat down on a blue scooter and bounced up and down on it. 'Nice,' he said.

'It's the only way to travel,' said Archie.

Charlie looked over at him. 'How long are you going to keep this up for?' he asked.

'The not-being-able-to-walk thing?' Archie shrugged. 'Not long. I'm starting to get bored.'

'Mrs Woodhouse will go mental,' said Billy.

'I'll say it was a miracle,' said Archie. 'I'll tell her I prayed to the Lord.' He looked up at the sky. 'Hallelujah!'

'You mad bastard,' laughed Charlie. He started his scooter but he had it in reverse and it crunched into the wall. 'Whoops,' he said.

'You guys follow me,' said Archie.

'Where are we going?' asked Billy.

'It's a magical mystery tour,' said Archie. He edged his scooter away from the wall and drove slowly through the car park. A barrier blocked the entrance but there was plenty of room to pass on the scooter. He drove onto the pavement and twisted around to check that Charlie and Billy were following him. Charlie waved. 'Yee ha!' he shouted.

Archie drove along the pavement. It was cold and a stiff breeze was blowing so there were few pedestrians around. He headed to a crossroads and drove to the crossing. He leaned over to press the crossing button and his two companions rolled up as the red man turned to green. They crossed the road and Archie headed towards the promenade. Seagulls whirled overhead as Archie pulled up at another crossing. Two modern grey trams rattled by and then they got the green signal and they drove across. Off to the right were the town's three piers jutting into the sea and the iconic Blackpool Tower.

Archie turned to drive along the promenade towards the nearest pier. It was the South Pier, the youngest of the three structures sticking out into the sea. It had opened in 1893 and had originally been called the Victoria Pier. The pier's amusement arcades were a firm favourite with children. The North Pier was built in 1863, and shortly afterwards the Central Pier was opened. The Central Pier had a 33 metre Ferris wheel, bars and theatre while the North Pier was more traditional with a Gypsy palm reader, a Victorian tea room and a carousel.

Despite the autumn chill there were still plenty of holidaymakers, most of them bundled up in warm coats and wearing covid masks. The tide was out and the featureless sand spread for almost half a mile. A line of donkeys stood shivering at the foot of a set of steps leading down from the promenade. A big man in a sheepskin jacket and a Russian fur hat was standing next to a sign offering donkey rides. They drove by a family, mum and dad and two toddlers, all bundled up against the cold, with Manchester United scarfs, wool hats and covid masks.

The children spotted the three scooters and pointed excitedly. 'I want one, dad!' shouted the boy. He was wearing a covid mask but had looped it under his chin.

'Me too! Can we have a go, daddy?' shouted the girl.

'They're for old people,' said the father.

Archie waved as he drove by.

'But they're fun!' shouted the little girl.

'Big fun!' shouted Charlie. 'But you've another seventy years before you'll be ready for one!' He blew the girl a kiss as he went by and she laughed.

'I want one, daddy!' shouted the girl.

Archie looked over his shoulder. Charlie and Billy were laughing. Archie punched the air with his fist and howled like a wolf. He almost lost control of his scooter and narrowly missed scraping it along a wall. Charlie and Billy roared with laughter and Archie flashed them a V-sign.

There were a few holidaymakers braving the chill wind blowing off the sea but Archie had no problem avoiding them. He took the scooter up to its top speed and his eyes were soon watering. When he reached the entrance to the south pier, his cheeks were damp with tears. He waited for Charlie and Billy to join him and grinned when he saw their eyes were also watering.

'Fucking brilliant,' said Charlie, wiping his cheeks with the back of his hand. 'How much fun is this?'

'Beats walking,' said Billy. 'How fast were we going?'

'About ten miles an hour,' said Archie. 'Feels faster because you're on the pavement. You're supposed to stick to four miles an hour, but what are they gonna do? Give us a speeding ticket?' He pointed at the entrance. 'Right, let's head onto the pier.'

'Is it okay to go on with these?' asked Billy.

'Mate, we're disabled,' said Archie. 'We can go wherever we want.' He drove onto the pier and Charlie and Billy followed. There were a lot of people milling around the entrance but they moved out of the way to give the scooters room to pass. Archie waved regally as he drove into the amusement arcade. Elderly women wearing winter coats and covid masks were pumping coins into fruit machines and parents were watching their children operate cranes to grab at cuddly toys. A young couple were blasting away at digital zombies while their toddler cried in its pushchair. The air was filled with buzzing and bells ringing and children chattering excitedly. Archie weaved through the crowds, occasionally sounding his horn to announce his presence.

The far end of the amusement arcade opened onto the pier. There were booths left and right offering games of skill for children to win Chinese-made stuffed animals. Archie drove by. A bald man in a blue anorak wearing a clear plastic face shield held out three darts and offered him the chance to pop balloons. Archie grinned. 'Disabled, mate,' he said as he drove by.

He pulled up in front of a booth selling fish and chips and ordered three portions. He handed over a twenty pound note, told the young server to keep the change, and passed portions to Charlie and Billy. They drove over to the edge of the pier and parked facing the sea.

'This is the life,' said Billy, and he bit into a chip.

'You've been here before, right?' asked Archie.

'The pier? Not really. We don't really go out much.'

'Why not?'

Billy shrugged. 'I dunno. We just stay in and play dominoes. It's not as if we can afford the one armed bandits, is it?' He held up his fish and chips. 'And I certainly couldn't afford this.'

'You're skint?'

'I get the state pension and that's it. The company I worked for went bust a few years ago and the pension went bust with it.'

'That doesn't sound right.'

'Right or wrong, that's what happened. Now I don't have two pennies to rub together.'

'What about you, Charlie?' asked Archie.

'I was self-employed and never bothered with a pension. I just assumed I would work for ever.' He broke off a piece of battered cod and popped it into his mouth, then moaned with pleasure. He chewed and swallowed. 'Fuck me, that tastes good.'

'What about you, Archie?' asked Billy. 'You don't look like you're short of a bob or two.'

'You can't have any money, though,' said Charlie. 'That's the first thing the fuckers do, take all your money.'

'You're allowed twenty-three and a half grand, last time I checked,' said Archie.

Billy snorted. 'Chance'd be a fine thing,' he said,

'What about you, Archie?' asked Charlie. 'Have you got twenty-three and a half grand tucked away?'

Archie grinned over at him. 'Mate, how much I might or might not have tucked away is my business and my business only.' He waved a chip around. 'But I'll tell you one thing, the Government's never going to put a finger on my stash.'

He put the chip towards his mouth but a huge seagull beat him to it, sweeping down and grabbing it with its beak before flying off. 'Thieving bastard!' shouted Archie.

Billy and Archie burst into laughter and Archie grinned ruefully. 'Can't trust anybody these days.'

'But at least you were smart enough to put something by,' said Charlie. 'If I'd known I was going to live this long I'd have taken better care of my money.' He shrugged. 'No use crying over spilled milk.' He popped a piece of fish into his mouth.

Archie waved his hand at the sea. 'Come on, it's not too bad. We live by the ocean, free room and board, there are people a lot worse off than us.'

'Easy for you to say, Archie,' said Billy. 'You're a newbie. Wait until you've been here a few years.'

Charlie snorted. 'Fuck that. You know the average length of stay is in a care home like ours? Just over two years. And half of the residents die in the first year.'

'You're a right little ray of sunshine, aren't you?' said Archie.

'Like Billy said, you're a newbie.'

'How long have you been there?'

'Just over three years.'

Archie looked at Billy. 'And you?"

'Just under two.' Billy threw a chip at a seagull. The bird fluttered its wings and caught it before flying off. 'I fucking hate it.'

'We all hate it,' said Charlie. 'No one would choose to live there.'

'Well I did, in a way,' said Archie. 'I mean, I didn't choose it, but I wanted out of my old place.'

'Where was that?' asked Charlie.

'Middle of Peston,' said Archie. 'Now that was a shit-hole. At least here we can get a bit of sea air, even walk on the beach if we want. You guys should count your blessings.'

They finished their fish and chips, then drove their scooters back onto the promenade. Charlie took the lead. 'Last one home's a wanker!' he shouted. Billy and Archie gave chase. Billy rocked back and forth as if that would edge up his speed, but Archie figured that wind resistance was more of an issue so he crouched down over the handlebars. By the time they reached the turn-off, Billy was a good fifty feet behind but Archie had gained on Charlie. He tried to overtake but Charlie swerved to the side to block him. Archie cursed and had to brake to avoid hitting Charlie. Charlie whooped and punched the air.

Archie accelerated but Charlie had already reached the entrance to the care home's car park.

Connolly was leaning against the wall smoking a cigarette and his eyes narrowed as he watched the three men drive up on the mobility scooters. He had his face shield flipped back and his covid mask pulled under his chin.

'Oy, you can't be driving them!' he shouted.

'Why not?' asked Charlie, climbing off his scooter. 'They're for residents, aren't they?'

'For disabled residents, like him.' He jabbed his cigarette at Archie. 'He's okay, he's disabled, but you and Billy, there's nothing wrong with you.'

Archie parked his scooter next to Charlie's and stood up. He stretched and grinned at the look of confusion on Connolly's face.

Billy parked and looked over at Connolly, who was staring open-mouthed at Archie. 'What's the problem?' Billy asked Archie.

'No problem,' said Archie.

Charlie headed towards the door and Archie followed him. He gestured at the wheelchair. 'I won't be needing that any more, Mr Connolly,' he said. 'Looks like the sea air's doing me the world of good.'

'Are you taking the piss?' scowled Connolly.

Archie stopped and spread out his hands. 'Why would I do that, Mr Connolly? You should be pleased. I can walk again. It's a miracle.' He raised his hands up into the air. 'The Lord be praised.'

Billy came up behind Archie and patted him on the back. 'You're a madman,' he said.

They walked into the home with Connolly glaring daggers at them.

'Thanks for that, Archie,' said Billy. 'I haven't that much fun since I don't know when.'

Charlie nodded in agreement. 'Yeah, that was fun. Maybe we should go full-time disabled.'

CHAPTER 10

Sally walked over with three plates of food on a plastic tray. She was wearing full PPE and her visor was misting over. 'Here's your dinner, gentlemen,' she said cheerily. She placed the tray on the table. Archie sneered as he looked at the watery cream sauce with lumps in it, mashed potato that was so smooth it could only have been instant, and yellowish boiled cabbage.

'Sally, love, what is this?' asked Archie.

Sally put one of the plates in front of Charlie. 'It's chicken au something or other,' she said. 'It's French.'

She put the other two plates in front of Billy and Archie, then gathered up the tray.

Archie prodded one of the lumps with his knife. 'Is there a cat living here?'

Sally frowned.

'A cat,' said Archie. 'Four legs and fur and whiskers. Is there one in the home?'

'Pets aren't allowed,' she said. 'Why?'

'Because something's thrown up on my plate. Sally, love, I wouldn't feed this to someone on death row.'

Billy grinned. 'Well, strictly speaking…that's sort of where we are.'

Charlie nodded. 'Death's doorstep. He put a forkful of the mush into his mouth and shrugged. 'I've had worse.'

Archie shook his head in disgust as Sally walked away. 'I can't eat this shit,' he said.

'You get used to it,' said Billy.

'I don't want to get used to it,' said Archie. He dropped his knife and fork onto the plate and pushed it away. 'Seriously, we should do something about this.'

'Do what?' asked Billy. 'It's run by the council. You can complain all you want but they won't do anything.'

Charlie waved his fork at Archie's plate. 'Are you serious, you're not going to eat it?'

'Help yourself, mate,' said Archie.

Charlie reached over to pick up Archie's plate, then he scraped the food onto his own.

Archie sighed and leaned back in his chair. Connolly was sitting at a table by the wall, feeding an elderly man who was clearly blind. As Archie watched, Connolly spat onto the man's potato and mashed the phlegm in with a spoon before scoping some up and holding it out. He said something and the man opened his mouth, revealing half a dozen yellowed teeth. Connolly slid the spoon between the man's lips and the man bit down on it.

'Don't stare,' whispered Billy. 'You don't want him mad at you.'

'Why does nobody say anything?' asked Archie.

'You don't fuck with the staff because if the staff fuck with you you'll know you've been fucked,' said Charlie.

Connolly looked over at their table and both men quickly averted their eyes.

'If he gets on your case, he'll do more than spit in your food,' said Billy. 'Best just ignore what he does.'

'We could complain to the council,' said Archie.

'The council doesn't give a shit,' said Charlie. 'No one gives a shit. During the covid thing, they were dropping like flies here and no one from the council even bothered to come around. Even the doctors stopped coming. Undertakers refused to set foot inside, the staff here had to take the bodies out the back.'

'It was bad?' asked Archie.

'It was a fucking nightmare,' said Charlie. 'Half the residents died.'

'More than half,' said Billy. 'The undertakers were coming pretty much every day. They gave the staff body bags and the staff would pack the bodies and carry them outside to the undertakers. They were falling like ninepins. They had none of that TCP.'

'PPE, he means,' said Charlie. Masks and gloves and shit. They had none of that. One of the residents went into hospital for her diabetes. What was her name?'

Billy nodded. 'Molly.'

'Yeah, Molly,' said Charlie, punctuating his words with jabs of his fork. 'She used to be a librarian. They had her in for three nights and then they sent her home with the virus. She was coughing and couldn't breathe but they wouldn't send an ambulance to take her back in. And the GP wouldn't come out and check on her. She died and then other residents started to get sick.'

'What about you guys?' asked Archie. 'Did you catch it?'

Both men nodded. 'We got it,' said Charlie. 'We were as sick as shit but we got through it. To be honest, I've had worse flu. But it hit Billy harder.'

Billy grimaced at the memory. 'Yeah, I was on an incubator for two weeks.'

'Ventilator,' corrected Charlie.

'It fucked up my lungs,' said Billy. 'But I was one of the lucky ones. They didn't give a fuck. Management didn't get any gear in. The GP wouldn't visit, the hospitals wouldn't send ambulances. They wanted us to die here. It was a cull. That's what it was. A fucking cull.'

'At least you pulled through,' said Archie.

'Sure, the doctors and nurses at the Vic were brilliant. They saved my life, no question. But it was those same doctors and nurses who sent Molly back here with the virus.'

'Yeah, you didn't see us standing in the street clapping for the NHS,' said Charlie. 'Not when we saw what was happening here. I sometimes wonder if it was a conspiracy to get rid of the old folk.'

'To save money?'

Charlie nodded. 'It costs the council thousands for every resident. How does it not make economic sense to let the grim reaper do his stuff?'

Archie chuckled. 'Well this got depressing fast, didn't it?' He stood up. 'I'm going to have a smoke in the garden.'

'What about your ice cream?' asked Billy.

'What ice cream?'

'Dessert. It's chocolate ice cream today.'

'You can have mine,' said Archie. He headed to the door, avoiding eye contact with Connolly who was tapping the spoon against the blind man's chin.

Charlie and Billy watched him go. 'What do you think?' asked Charlie.

'He's a laugh,' said Billy.

'Yeah, well see if he's laughing in a month or two.'

'He livens the place up, nothing wrong with that. Let's face it, I'd rather have Archie than another one of the Walking Dead. At least he doesn't dribble when he eats.'

'Just be careful what you say to him, that's all. He's an unknown quantity.'

'I'm not stupid, Charlie.'

'I never said you were. We just need to be careful we don't say anything untoward.'

'I won't,' said Billy.

'I'm serious,' said Charlie.

Billy looked across the table, his eyes narrowing. 'So am I.'

CHAPTER 11

Kate Dolan turned the volume up on her Sony Walkman and nodded her head in time to The Lion Sleeps Tonight. She had made the tape herself and the Tight Fit song was her favourite. She had been the first of her friends to own a Sony Walkman, her parents had bought it for her twenty-first birthday present. It was amazing, it meant she could take her own music wherever she wanted. She recorded the songs she wanted from her radio or her record player onto a cassette player and then played the cassettes on the Walkman. Using headphones meant the sound was as loud as if she was playing her record player at full volume, but nobody else could hear. It was like having her own private concert.

She peered down the road. The bus was due within the next ten minutes, but she knew from experience that the timetable was more guesswork than anything. She looked to her left and realised that a car had stopped. It was a blue Ford Escort. A man was winding down the window and smiling at her. He was middle-aged with longish blond hair cut in a mullet. She assumed he was going to ask for directions so she took off her headphones.

'Hey, love, there's no buses running,' said the man.

She frowned at him. 'What?'

'I said there's no buses running. There's a strike.'

Kate's frown deepened. 'I saw one going the other other way just a few minutes ago.'

The man nodded. 'Yeah, that's going back to the depot. They've been talking about it on the radio. It's some sort of strike. They want more money for overtime or something.'

Kate looked at her bright red Casio watch. It was just after six and she had promised to meet her friends at the White Swan and then they were going to go from there to a nightclub in Birmingham. If she was late they'd go without her. The nearest phone box was a quarter of a mile away so all she could do was to go home and get the number of the pub from directory enquiries and then call them.

'Where are you going, love?' asked the man.

'Pub called the White Swan,' she said. 'Four miles down the road.'

'That's on my way, I can drop you if you want. It's no trouble.' He smiled and shrugged. 'Totally up to you.'

'Yeah, okay, thanks,' said Kate, She hurried around to the passenger side and opened the door. There was a pine air freshener in the shape of a Christmas tree hanging from the rear view mirror. She climbed in and pulled the door shut.

'Seat belt,' he said.

'Okay,' she said.

'You have to wear them by law starting next year, so I'm getting into the habit now,' he said. He put the car in gear and drove forward. 'So what are your plans for tonight?'

'Girls night out,' she said. 'Few drinks in the pub and then we're off to Birmingham to hit the clubs.'

'Sounds like a fun night,' he said. 'So you've no boyfriend?'

'Why do you say that?'

The man shrugged. 'If I had a pretty girl like you, I wouldn't be letting her go out clubbing without me.'

Kate laughed. 'It's the eighties, girls have just as much right to have a night out as guys.'

'Sure,' said the man. 'And you probably don't want to get tied down at your age. What are you? Twenty-two?'

'Next birthday,' she said. 'What about you. How old are you?'

'How old do you think?'

She squinted at him. 'Fifty?'

'Bloody hell, do you think I look fifty?'

She nodded. 'Yeah.'

'I'm still in my forties. My early forties if you must know.'

'You look like my dad, and he's fifty-three.'

The man looked unhappy so she figured she should try and get back on his good side as there was still some way to go to the White Swan. She hugged her handbag to her stomach, 'You know, they said the world might end today,' she said.

The man laughed. 'Who said?'

'It was in the papers yesterday. All nine of the planets are lined up on the same side of the sun.'

The man frowned, clearly not understanding her. 'What?'

'You know how all the planets go around the sun, right. Mercury, Venus, the Earth, Mars, all the way out to Pluto.' The man nodded. 'Well today all of those planets are on one side of the sun and some scientists say that the stress will tear the solar system apart.'

'That sounds pretty serious.'

She looked at her watch again. 'It's after six now, if anything bad was going to happen it'd have happened already,' she said. She smiled. 'I'm too young to die, anyway.'

'Everybody dies sometime,' said the man.

Kate looked out of the window. It looked like it might rain.

'I suppose so,' she said. 'No suppose so about it,' said the man. 'Death and taxes are the only two things in life guaranteed. Oh, look, I should have mentioned this before, I have to pick something up from a pal. It'll only take a few minutes.'

'Sure, that's okay,' she said.

'It's some boxes of clothes and stuff that he wants me to drop off at a charity shop. I'll just pick them up and put them in the boot and then I'll drop you off.'

'Yeah, that's fine,' said Kate.

He indicated a left turn and turned off the main road. He drove through a council estate and then by an industrial estate. 'Are we going to a shop?' she asked.

'It's a house,' he said. 'Not far now.'

They drove for another five minutes down a quiet road with detached houses either side, then turned into what looked like a council estate with shabbier homes and flat-roofed pubs some of which were topped with barbed wire. Kate frowned and looked at her watch. He had said it would only take a few minutes but it was now looking like a major detour.

'Nearly there,' he said as if reading her mind. 'We'll be back on the main road in no time.'

He took a left and they were in a cul-de-sac of small detached houses. The garage door was up at one of the houses and he drove inside. The manoeuvre took her by surprise and she looked around nervously. 'What are you doing?' she asked.

He flashed her a beaming smile. 'My pal said to drive in and he'd put the boxes in my boot. You can stay where you are, I won't be long.'

'Okay,' she said, but she still felt uneasy.

He climbed out of the car, went over to the garage door and pulled it down, then switched on an overhead light. Katie realised then that there was something terribly wrong but she stayed where she was, clutching her handbag. She heard his shoes crunch on the concrete as he walked around the car, then he pulled open the passenger side. 'Maybe you could come inside and help me with the boxes,' he said.

'You said your friend would bring them out.'

'Yes, well maybe we could give him a hand. Come on, don't be a spoilsport. I'm giving you a free ride, aren't I?'

She reluctantly got out of the car. She flinched as he slammed the door shut, the sound hitting her like an explosion in the confines of the garage. She was close to tears and she hugged her handbag as if her life depended on it. He put a hand on her shoulder and guided her to an internal door that led into the house. He opened it and let her through first. It opened into a small kitchen and another door led to a hallway. Part of her wanted to run for the front door but it might be locked and if she ran then he'd know that she knew something was wrong and providing they were both smiling then nothing bad was going to happen. 'Just go into the hall and up the stairs,' he said. 'Everything's going to be fine.'

She wanted to beg him to let her go, to not hurt her, but she knew that as soon as she said anything like that it would make it real. For the moment she could just about hold on to the belief that the friend was upstairs with the boxes that he was going to take to a charity shop.

She went slowly up the stairs. He followed her. 'First door on the left,' he said.

She pushed open the door and her breath caught in her throat when she saw a double mattress on the floor covered with a grey blanket. Next to the mattress was a wooden chair and on the chair were two coils of rope and two pairs of handcuffs and a weird looking chain with a red ball on it. On the floor by the chair were bottles of different sizes and what looked like a rounders bat. Kate stopped. Her whole body was trembling. 'Please don't hurt me,' she whispered.

'I won't hurt you if you do exactly as I say,' said the man.

She turned to face him and her heart lurched when she saw the large knife he was holding. He closed the door and waved the knife at her. 'Take off your clothes, darling. You can put them on the chair.'

Tears began to run down her face as she put her handbag on the chair and began to undress. She stripped down to her underwear and stood with her arms crossed and her legs pressed together.

'Everything, darling,' he said. 'Don't make me tell you again.'

The next three or four hours passed in a blur. She didn't fight him, she didn't resist, she just let him get on with it. Her way of dealing with it was just to pretend it was happening to someone else, to send her mind to a happier place, with her family, with her friends. Some of the things he did hurt her but even the pain faded eventually. Sometimes he asked her to say things and she did, she repeated them in a flat emotionless voice, just telling him what he wanted to hear. He was the best, she loved him, she needed him to fuck her harder, she wanted his baby. Everything he wanted her to say, she said.

About an hour after she had entered the room, she realised that she would never leave it alive. He wasn't going to let her go, he was going to kill her. She realised it and she accepted it because by then it was all happening to somebody else. She was sad that she was going to die but she wasn't scared, she just wanted him to leave her alone and if death meant that he would stop hurting her then death was something to be welcomed.

When death finally came he was naked on top of her, he was bathed in sweat and flecked with her blood and he had his hands around her throat. She tried to pull his hands away but by then she had no strength left. In her last seconds she closed her eyes and thought about her mum and dad and then there was nothing, just peace.

CHAPTER 12

Billy was placing a double seven down and Charlie was grinning when Archie walked over to their table. Charlie placed his final tile, a seven and a three.

'Shit, I thought you were out of sevens,' said Billy.

'That's what I wanted you to think,' said Charlie.

Billy turned over his tiles and Charlie added up the points.

'Okay if I sit in?' asked Archie.

'Sure,' said Charlie.

Archie grabbed a chair from a neighbouring table and sat down. 'So what's the game?' he asked.

Billy turned all the tiles face down and began swirling them around. 'We play a version called Sebastopol,' he said. 'You take seven tiles and the double nine starts. If no one has the double nine, we keep taking tiles from the boneyard until one of us have it.'

'The boneyard?' repeated Archie.

'That's what the pool is called,' said Charlie, picking seven tiles at random and placing them in front of him. Archie and Billy did the same.

'Anyone got it?' asked Billy.

Charlie and Archie shook their heads. They began drawing tiles and it was Archie who picked the double-nine. He placed it in the middle of the table.

'Right,' said Billy. 'Now we take it in turns clockwise, so Charlie is next to play. The next four dominoes have to have a nine and they have to be placed on each side and each end. That makes four ends which can be added to. But you can't start adding to the lines until all four are in place.'

'Bloody hell, this is complicated,' said Archie, running a hand through his hair.

'Nah, it's easy enough,' said Charlie. He put a nine on one end of the double nine. If you can't play, you take an extra domino. First one to play all his dominoes is the winner.'

Billy placed a tile at the other end of the double-nine and looked over at Archie. Archie shook his head and picked up a tile. Charlie grinned and played a second nine.

A pizza delivery man in a high-vis jacket appeared at the window. He was in his early twenties with a baseball cap bearing the pizza company's logo and another logo on his covid mask. He was holding two large pizza boxes.

Archie waved at him and opened the window.

'Archie Jennings?' asked the delivery guy.

'That's me,' said Archie. He took the pizza boxes from him. put them on the table and handed the man a twenty pound note. 'Keep the change, mate,' he said. The man thanked him and walked off as Archie closed the window.

Charlie and Billy stared at the boxes in astonishment. 'You are fucking kidding me,' said Charlie.

'What?' asked Archie. He flipped open the lid of the top box. It was a pepperoni pizza, cut into eight slices.

'You can't do this,' said Charlie.

'I already did,' said Archie. He held out the box. 'Help yourself.'

'You are a madman,' said Charlie,. He reached over and grabbed a slice. Billy did the same.

Charlie sat down and took a large bite, smearing tomato sauce over his upper lip. He sighed contentedly and chewed.

'I haven't had pizza for years,' said Billy. 'Not real pizza, anyway. They do a pastry thing with tinned tomato and cheese slices on it and call it pizza but it isn't.' He took a bite and grinned. 'Now this is pizza.'

Raja came over to their table, frowning. He pointed at the boxes. 'What's this?' he asked.

'Pizza,' said Archie. 'A large circle of flat bread baked with cheese, tomatoes and sometimes meat and vegetables spread on top.'

'I know what pizza is, Archie.'

'You asked and I answered, mate.'

'You can't go ordering pizzas.'

'Why not?'

'You just can't. There are rules. We can't have food delivery people walking in and out.'

'He didn't walk in or out,' said Archie. 'He passed them through the window from an acceptable social distance.'

Raja shook his head. 'Archie, rules are rules.'

Archie smiled amiably. 'Raja, mate, let me ask you a question. Are we prisoners or are we guests?'

'You're residents,' said Raja, patiently.

'So not prisoners, right? We live here. This is our home.' He nodded encouragingly.

'I suppose so,' said Raja.

'And you are paid to take care of us.'

Raja folded his arms defensively. 'Yes, but not by you. The council pays.'

Archie nodded. 'Yes, the council pays. The council pays YOU to take care of US. And at the moment you're not. Not food-wise, anyway. The food is shit here. We know it's shit and you know it's shit, so if I want to order pizza I'll bloody well order pizza.' He held out the box. 'Now do you want a slice or not?'

Raja looked down at the pizza, then slowly smiled. 'It does look good,' he said.

'Fucking tastes good, too,' said Charlie, wiping his mouth with his sleeve.

Raja chuckled and took a piece. 'Just don't let Mrs Woodhouse catch you,' he said, and walked away.

Charlie had finished his first slice and took another. Archie put down the box and picked up the second one. He flipped it open to reveal a cheese and tomato pizza. He took it around the room, offering it to the residents. Most just looked at him blankly but several did beam and take a slice. He approached an elderly man in a wheelchair. Most of the man's left leg was missing. He grinned up at Archie, His teeth were yellowed but his tongue appeared to be covered in white fur.

'Hi mate, fancy a slice of pizza?' asked Archie, holding out the box.

The man took a slice. 'Thanks, Bob,' he said. 'How's your mum?'

'My name's Archie, mate.'

The man frowned up at him. 'Why would you say that, Bob?'

'Seriously, mate. I'm Archie.'

The man laughed. 'Always the jokester, Bob.' He held up the pizza slice. 'You make this?'

'No, I ordered it. Enjoy.'

Archie did a full circuit of the room and the box was soon empty. By the time he got back to his table, Billy and Charlie had devoured most of the second box. He sat down and took a slice himself. 'All right, lads?' he asked.

'Who the hell are you, Archie Jennings?' said Charlie.

'He's a breath of fresh air, that's what he is,' said Billy.

'Or maybe the wind of change,' said Archie. 'We might be sitting in Death's Waiting Room but that doesn't mean we can't have a laugh or two.'

CHAPTER 13

Archie had set his phone alarm to wake him at seven-thirty but he was already awake and staring at the ceiling when it rang. He rolled over and turned it off. He opened his curtains and stared through the window at the home's collection of rubbish bins, colour-coded according to their contents. A tortoiseshell cat was sitting on one of the bins and it stared back at him with unblinking green eyes.

Archie turned away and slowly got down on his knees, then leaned forward and did twenty slow press-ups before rolling onto his back and doing sit-ups. He got to his feet and spent a few minutes stretching and touching his toes, then dropped and did another twenty press-ups. In his youth he'd played rugby and tennis and in his forties and fifties he'd been a keen jogger, often running with his wife. His wife had passed away and he hated running alone so at aged sixty-five he had taken up golf, though after a few months he'd realised that while he enjoyed the walk, hitting balls with a stick wasn't that much fun. He'd decided that a dog would be a better walking companion than a set of clubs so had taken a Spaniel cross from a dog shelter and spent eight happy years before she had died of cancer, just like his wife. He had never considered replacing his wife and he felt the same way about the dog, so exercise for the past two years had been a morning work out, a combination of press-ups, sit-ups and basic yoga.

He was breathing heavily when he finished, then he shaved, showered and dressed and went down to breakfast. Billy and Charlie were already at their table. An oxygen cylinder stood by Billy's chair. Archie looked at it as he sat down. 'Not going scuba diving, are you mate?'

Billy patted his chest. 'I was a bit short of breath last night so I've been taking extra oxygen.'

'Are you okay?

Billy forced a smile. 'Forty fags a day for forty years or more. But it was the covid that fucked up my lungs. Some days are worse than others. The Doc says it's stress related. I still like the odd cigarette, mind.'

'Yeah. I tried to give up,' said Archie. 'But at the end of the day, I like to smoke.'

'Me too,' said Charlie. 'But I packed it in.'

'Health reasons?'

Charlie shook his head. 'Couldn't afford it. Price went through the roof. I tried roll ups but my hands shook so much that I spilled most of the tobacco.' He held out his hands and he grimaced at the way they trembled.

'That's something we've got in common,' said Archie. 'Getting old sucks.'

'Yeah, but it's better than the alternative,' said Billy.

Charlie was buttering a slice of pale toast. On the plate in front of him was a pile of anaemic scrambled eggs, two hot dog sausages and half a tomato. 'They say that using those tanks just makes it worse,' he said, gesturing at Billy's cylinder.

'Yeah?' said Billy. 'Remind me again where you got your degree in medicine.'

Charlie waved his knife at Billy. 'I'm just saying, sometimes when doctors interfere, they get it wrong. Look at the ventilators they used when covid kicked off. Pretty much everyone they put on a ventilator died.'

'I was on a ventilator, Charlie.'

'Exactly. And now your lungs are fucked. It's like glasses.'

Sally brought over two breakfasts one for Billy and one for Archie. Archie shook his head at the watery eggs but Sally flashed him a warning look so he just nodded and flashed her a smile.

'Glasses?' he said to Charlie.

'Glasses,' repeated Charlie. He waved his knife at Archie. 'Your eyesight starts to go when you're forty or fifty, so what do they do?

They tell you to wear glasses but glasses make your eyes lazy so your eyesight gets worse and you have to get stronger and stronger glasses.'

'You've lost me, Charlie,' said Archie.

'The ones who got covid bad got put on ventilators. The ventilators did what the lungs are supposed to do, get oxygen into the system. But once you've got a machine doing the job, the lungs don't have to work. So they stop. It's obvious, innit. I could see that, why couldn't the doctors? It was only when they stopped using the ventilators that people stopped dying. Like Billy said before, it was a cull. A fucking cull. Billy and were lucky to survive.' His eyes narrowed. 'What about you?'

'I didn't get it,' said Archie. 'Not that I know of. But they tested me before they transferred me here and said that I had the antibodies, so who knows. I had a bit of a cough before the first lockdown so maybe I had it then, but it was just a cough.'

'You were one of the lucky ones,' said Billy. 'At our age, it's no fucking joke.'

'What about the place you were at?' asked Charlie. 'How many died?'

Archie shrugged. 'It wasn't that bad. They shut it down pretty quickly and banned all visitors. Didn't worry me, I never had visitors anyway. They had all the right gear so they were on top of it.'

'Well it was a fucking nightmare here,' said Charlie. 'They had a blanket DNR rule.'

'DNR?

'Do not resuscitate,' said Charlie. 'Basically if your heart stopped you were on your own, they wouldn't try to bring you back.'

'It was all planned,' said Billy. 'They wanted rid of the old folk. Every one of us that died saved them tens of thousands of pounds a year.'

'But you're saying that your place took care of you?' Charlie asked Archie.

'They did their best,' said Archie. He spread margarine onto a slice of toast but it was too hard and the bread tore and he cursed. 'If they don't get the toast sorted soon, I'll buy a bloody toaster myself,' he said. He dropped the bread onto his plate and piled on eggs, then added a squirt of ketchup. The sauce didn't improve the taste much but it made them at least palatable. He poured himself a cup of weak tea and he cursed again. 'Would it kill them to put in an extra tea-bag?'

Charlie laughed. 'You need to relax,' he said. 'You've only just got here. I was here six months before I let it get to me.'

Archie forced a smile. 'Yeah, you're right. I should try to go with the flow. What is it they say in AA? God grant me the serenity to accept the things I cannot change, courage to change the things I can, and the wisdom to know the difference.'

'Are you in AA?' asked Billy.

Archie shook his head. 'Hell no, I love my beer too much for that. But I get the sentiment. There's no point in trying to change something that can't be changed.' He looked around the room and shook his head. 'This place doesn't need changing, it needs razing to the ground.' He took his tablets from his pocket and swallowed three, washing them down with tea.

'See now I've never understood that expression,' said Billy, spearing a sausage with his fork. 'How can you lift something to the ground?'

Archie laughed but then realised that Billy was serious. 'It's a totally different word, mate,' he said. 'Raze. R-A-Z-E. Not raise, R-A-I-S-E. It means to destroy.'

Billy nodded. 'Thanks for the English lesson,' he said. 'You seem pretty smart for a butcher.'

'Retired butcher,' said Archie. 'I was never that smart at school, I left when I was sixteen, but I've always been a reader. I'll read anything, me.'

'Me too,' said Billy.

Charlie pulled a face. 'I was never one for books,' he said. 'Unless they had pictures in them.' He finished the last of his eggs and popped the final piece of toast into his mouth. 'Are you up for dominoes or are you taking your scooter out for a ride?'

Archie looked through the window. The sky overhead was filled with grey clouds. 'Looks like it's going to piss down,' he said. 'So dominoes sounds good.'

'We play for points,' said Charlie. 'There's no money involved.'

'But he still cheats,' said Billy.

Archie laughed. 'Good to know.'

'Billy's just a sore loser,' said Charlie. He drained his cup of tea, took hold of his walking stick and used it to get to his feet. 'The only reason I play with him is because they're his dominoes.'

He headed out. Archie and Billy finished their teas, then Billy bent down and retrieved his box of dominoes from under his chair. He put on his mask and picked up his oxygen cylinder and they followed him to the day room.

There were only two chairs at the table by the window, so Archie grabbed a third from a neighbouring table. When he sat down, Billy had placed all the dominoes face down on the table and was mixing them up. When he finished, Archie looked at them and frowned. 'You know you're missing one,' he said.

Billy screwed up his eyes. 'What?'

Archie leaned back in his chair. 'There are fifty-five dominoes in a double-nine set, right? But you've got fifty-four tiles on the table.'

'You counted them?' Charlie asked.

'Sure.'

'How do you do that?' asked Billy. 'How do you count so fast?'

'I just do. I've got a trick memory or something. Anyway, you're a tile short.'

Billy scratched the back of his head. 'Yeah, I dropped them this morning. It'll be on the floor in my room.'

Billy began to get to his feet but Archie beat him to it. 'No point in carrying your scuba gear around, I'll get it,' he said.

Billy settled back in his chair. 'Okay. Room 212.'

Archie flashed Billy a thumbs up and left the room. He took the stairs and hurried along the corridor to Billy's room. He opened it and stepped inside. It was identical in size and layout to his own. A dressing table and wardrobe to the left, a single bed and an easy chair to the right, with a door leading to a shower room. There was a small music centre on the dressing table with a dozen or so CDs in a pile. Archie went over and flicked through them. Roxy Music. Elton John. Dire Straits. Queen. Archie smiled to himself. Billy's taste in music was pretty much the same as his own, stuck in the seventies. He pulled open the top drawer and his smile widened when he saw that Billy's underwear and socks were neatly folded and colour coordinated. 'Birds of a feather, mate,' Archie whispered, and closed the drawer.

He turned around and looked at the bed with its single pillow in a black and white striped pillowcase and a dark green duvet. Archie put a hand on the bed to steady himself and then went down on his knees. He peered under the bed and immediately saw the domino. 'Come here you little bugger,' he said and groped for it. It was just out of reach, no matter how he stretched, so he sighed and lowered himself down until he was lying on the carpet. He reached out with his left hand and managed to get his fingertips to it, then slowly pulled it towards him. He grunted as his fingers slipped off the tile. He twisted his head to the side and stretched out again. His eyes opened in surprise when he saw the envelope taped to the bottom of the bed. He seized the domino and then reached up and grabbed the envelope.

He rolled out from under the bed and pushed himself up onto his knees. He tossed the domino onto the duvet and looked at the envelope. It was padded, creased in several places and dotted with stains. He opened it and looked inside. He frowned and tipped the contents onto the duvet. He looked down at eighteen smaller envelopes, each about three inches long and two inches wide. On each envelope was a name and date, written in capital letters. He picked up one of the envelopes. KATE. March 10, 1982. The flap wasn't stuck down and Archie opened it. He tipped up the envelope and shook it. A lock of blonde hair slipped out and dropped onto his palm. It was about three inches long, slightly wavy and appeared to be naturally blonde rather than dyed. The hair was kept together with a small piece of sellotape at one end. Archie raised the hair to his face and sniffed it. He put the lock of hair back in the envelope and picked up another one. This one had CAROL and the date January 27, 2002. Archie lifted the flap and tapped the envelope against his palm. Another lock of blonde hair fell out. The ends had been cut neatly and stuck together with sellotape. Archie frowned as he looked at the hair and then at the pile of envelopes on the duvet. He jumped as he heard the door slam behind him. He looked over his shoulder and saw Charlie and Billy glaring at him. Charlie was holding his stick like a club. Billy had taken off his mask but was holding his cylinder above his head as if he was getting ready to throw it at Archie. Archie dropped the hair and the envelope on the bed and struggled to his feet. 'What's up, lads?' he said, his voice trembling. He picked up the domino, held it out and forced a smile. 'I found it.'

Billy nodded at the pile of envelopes on the duvet. 'Looks like that's not the only thing you found.' He stepped forward, preparing to bring the cylinder crashing down on Archie.

Archie raised his hands defensively. 'Mate, hold your horses.'

Charlie took a step towards him, raising his stick higher.

'I'm serious, mate, there's no need for this,' said Archie. 'I need to show you something.'

'You don't need to show us anything,' said Charlie.

'We've seen everything we need to see,' said Billy.

Archie shook his head. 'Trust me, this you're going to want to see.'

Billy and Charlie looked at each other.

'Just give me a couple of minutes and you'll see what I mean.' He took a step forward, his hands still up. 'Come to my room, I'll show you.'

Charlie shook his head. 'You're not going anywhere.'

'Trust me. This you will want to see. What's the alternative? Beat me to death in Billy's room? How does that solve anything?'

Charlie stepped to the side but kept his stick raised. 'Okay, we'll go to your room. But don't try anything.'

'Bloody hell, Charlie, you've been watching too many gangster movies.' Archie put the hair back into the envelope and dropped it on

61

the duvet, then moved between the two men and opened the door. 'You'd better put that cylinder down, Billy,' he said. 'You'll do yourself a mischief.'

He went out into the corridor and headed for the stairs. The two men followed him. As they reached the stairs, Sally was coming up wearing full PPE gear and carrying a mop and bucket. 'What are you guys up to?' she asked.

'They were just showing me their rooms,' said Archie.

Sally stopped and looked at him suspiciously. 'I thought you had to stay on the ground floor,' she said. 'And weren't you in a wheelchair when you came in?'

'I'm on the mend, Sally love,' said Archie. 'It's probably all that healthy food you've been feeding me.'

He headed down the stairs and Billy and Charlie hurried after him. Sally turned to watch them go. 'Billy, if you're having trouble breathing you need to take it easy!' she called after them. 'And be careful carrying that cylinder around. You know how easy it is to put your back out.'

The three men hurried along the ground floor corridor and Sally sighed and headed up the stairs. 'They're as bad as kids sometimes,' she muttered to herself.

Archie reached the door to his room and waited for Billy and Charlie to catch up. 'You'd better not be wasting our time,' hissed Charlie.

'I'm not,' said Archie. He opened the door and stepped to the side to let them go in.

Charlie shook his head. 'You first.' He was still holding his walking stick in both hands.

Archie grinned. 'I'm not gonna be on my toes, mate,' he said. 'There's something I need to show you. Something the two of you will appreciate.' He held the door open but the two men stayed where they were. Archie sighed. 'Oh ye of little faith,' he said. He walked inside. They followed him and Charlie closed the door and stood with his back to it. Billy went over to the armchair and sat down. He was wheezing and he put on his mask and adjusted the oxygen flow. 'Are you all right, mate?' asked Archie.

'Don't worry about him,' said Charlie, hefting his walking stick. 'What do you want to show us?'

Archie patted Billy on the shoulder and went over to his bed. There was a small wooden box on the bedside cabinet, the size of a box of tissues. Different coloured woods had been used to make a geometrical pattern of triangles and squares. Archie sat down on the bed and opened the lid. Inside were two ballpoint pens, half a dozen keys on a four-leaf clover keyring, and a few coins. He emptied them out onto the bed.

'Wow, a real treasure trove,' said Charlie, his voice loaded with sarcasm.

Archie flashed him a tight smile, then reached into the box. He pressed a side panel and the bottom clicked open to reveal a secret compartment. Inside was a red velvet bag, its end closed with a gold cord. Archie took out the bag and put the box back on the bedside table. Charlie and Billy were watching wide-eyed. Archie loosened the gold cord, held out his left hand and emptied the contents of the bag onto his palm. There were nine rings. Six were wedding bands and three were gold with diamonds.

Charlie licked his lips. 'Fuck me sideways,' he whispered.

Attached to each ring was a small square piece of card, with writing on it. Archie stood up and walked over to Charlie., Charlie lowered his stick and took one of the rings. He squinted at the label while Archie went over to Billy. Billy frowned as he took one of the rings.

'Angela Clarke,' said Charlie. 'January tenth, 1998. Leeds.'

Archie sat back down on the bed. 'She cried and said she was pregnant,' he whispered. 'Said I could do anything to her if I'd just let her go.' He shrugged carelessly. 'Obviously I didn't.'

'Emma Kavanagh,' said Billy, reading the card he was holding. 'October the seventh. Manchester.'

Archie grinned. 'Now she was a looker. Drop dead gorgeous. I had her hooked up to a drip to keep her sedated for the best part of three days. He grinned at the two men. 'So it looks as if you and I have more in common than I thought, hey?'

Billy and Charlie looked at each other. 'It doesn't mean anything,' said Charlie.

'Oh come on, mate. They're trophies. Billy took hair, I took rings. What did you take?'

Charlie shook his head. 'I never took trophies.'

'Everyone takes trophies,' said Archie. 'Come on, you can tell me. Birds of a feather, that's what we are.'

'Those days are long gone,' said Charlie.

'Tell me about it,' said Archie. He held up the rings. 'But these, these trophies, they help you remember. You can relive the moment, whenever you want.'

Charlie smiled and tapped the side of his head. 'I remember everything,' he said. 'It's all in here.'

'Sure, but a trophy.' Archie shuddered with pleasure. 'A trophy is a direct connection to them.' He stood up and held out his hand. Charlie gave him back the ring. Billy did the same. Archie put them back into the bag, pulled the gold cord tight and then put it back into its hiding place. 'So are we good?' asked Archie.

Charlie looked at Billy. Billy nodded. 'I guess so,' said Charlie.

Archie grinned and nodded at Charlie's walking stick. 'Were you really going to belt me with that?'

Charlie shrugged. 'I hadn't decided. Maybe.'

'And then what? Split my skull open and claim what? That it was an accident?'

Charlie shrugged again. 'I hadn't thought that far ahead.'

They all jumped as the door was thrown open. Connolly stood in the doorway, his plastic face shield tilted back on his head. 'Is everything all right in here?' he asked. He was wearing Marigold gloves and carrying a toilet plunger.

'Just having a chat, Mr Connolly,' said Archie.

'You know the rules, guys,' said Connolly. 'No socialising in bedrooms.' He gestured with the plunger. 'If you want to socialise, do it in the day room.'

'We were just going out to the garden, Mr Connolly,' said Archie. 'Get a breath of fresh air.'

The three men headed down the corridor to the door that led to the garden. 'What an arsehole,' muttered Archie.

'Guy's a prick,' echoed Charlie. 'But Mrs Woodhouse likes him so he gets away with murder.'

'Not literally,' said Archie, flashing him a sideways look.

Charlie chuckled. 'No, not literally, squire.'

They walked out into the garden. It was about the size of a tennis court, bordered with a six-foot high hedge that hadn't been trimmed for a while. There were two trees, an apple and a beech, and half a dozen wooden benches around the perimeter. Most of the benches had small metal plaques on them, denoting a resident who had once enjoyed sitting there. Two ladies in wheelchairs had been parked at the far end of the garden, facing in the same direction, their wrinkled faces totally blank.

Archie took out a pack of cigarettes and lit one. He held out the pack to Billy but Billy shook his head and lifted the cylinder. 'Can't smoke while I've got this with me,' he said.

'Why did you bring it?' asked Archie. He waved his hand around. 'You've got all this lovely fresh air, why breathe out of a fucking can?'

Billy laughed and took off his mask. He put the cylinder on a bench and held out this hand. 'Yeah, give me one,' he said.

Archie held out the pack, Billy took a cigarette and Archie lit it for him with a cheap disposable lighter. Billy took a long drag, then blew smoke up at the sky and sighed contentedly.

Archie offered the pack to Charlie but he shook his head. 'I've given up,' he said. He lowered his voice and leaned towards Archie. 'How many?' he asked.

'Pack a day, maybe. Sometimes more, sometimes less.'

Charlie smiled thinly. 'How many rings, I meant.'

'Rings? Oh, rings. Nine.'

'Nine?' said Billy. He laughed. 'That's nothing. I did eighteen.'

'Yeah, but it's quality not quantity,' said Archie, flicking ash onto the grass.

'I did twenty-two,' said Charlie. 'But I started young.'

'And you never took trophies?'

'Never saw the point. It's asking to get caught.'

'The thing about trophies is that they help you remember.'

Billy nodded in agreement. 'Yeah. Brings it all back.'

'I don't need help, I can remember every one,' said Charlie. 'Like it happened yesterday. I can't remember whether or not I took my blood pressure medication but the details of what I did back then.' He shuddered with pleasure. 'That I remember. Every second of it.'

Billy and Archie finished their cigarettes and they went back to the day room. Billy placed the cylinder by his chair but didn't put on his mask. He grinned at Archie. 'I think that fag actually helped,' he said.

Archie put the missing domino on the table and sat down. 'They did say that smokers were less at risk from covid than non-smokers, remember?'

'Yeah, but he was smoking two packs a day when he got it, so I think that theory has been pretty much discredited,' said Charlie.

Charlie lowered himself onto his chair then leant his walking stick against the window sill. A female resident began screaming like a banshee at the far end of the room. Archie looked over as Everton and Sally hurried to her side. 'What's wrong with her?' asked Archie.

'She's one of Connolly's victims,' said Charlie. 'She was an MP, back in the day. Labour. They were going to put her in the House of Lords but then the Alzheimer's kicked in.'

The woman began to calm down as Everton and Sally talked to her.

Charlie swirled the dominoes around.

'The older I get, the more I forget,' said Archie. 'But as soon as I pick up one of the rings... it all comes back to me. Back in the day, I used to wear the rings after... usually on my little finger if it'd fit.'

Charlie finished mixing the dominoes and waved for Archie and Billy to choose their tiles. 'Always women?' he asked.

'Sure. You.'

'Of course. Always women. But I wasn't fussy about age or colour or anything like that. The youngest was seventeen, the oldest was a pensioner.'

Archie grinned. 'Grab a granny?'

'Nah, she was fit. I mean, yes, she was a grandmother but she was still fit.'

Archie stood his tiles up and shielded them with his hands. 'What about you, Billy?'

'I had a type,' said Billy.

Archie and Charlie winced. 'That's not good,' said Archie. 'That's never good.'

'I know, I know. That's the easiest way to get caught, but I had a thing about blonde hair.'

Archie nodded. 'Hence the trophies?'

'Yeah. Had to be a real blonde, too. If it was dyed, I had zero interest. But soft blonde hair, that always got my juices going.' He rubbed his hands together.

'Didn't the cops cotton on?' asked Archie.

Billy shook his head as he lined up his dominoes. 'No, my patch was the Midlands, the North of England all the way up to Scotland and across to Norfolk. I had about a third of the country to play with. And I made it a rule never to kill in the same police area consecutively. So if I did one in Manchester, I'd make sure the next one was in Newcastle or Durham. That way they never realised they had a serial.'

'Smart,' said Archie, nodding. He looked up from his dominoes. 'So we're all good?'

Charlie looked across at Billy. Billy nodded. Charlie mirrored the nod and then looked back at Archie. 'Yeah, birds of a feather.'

Archie grinned. 'Excellent,' he said. 'And to make my morning complete, I've got the double nine.'

He reached out and placed the double-nine domino on the table. Billy groaned. "Bastard.'

CHAPTER 14

Archie looked up as Sally carried a tray with three plates over to the table. She was wearing a hairnet and an N95 mask and had a face screen pulled down. Archie grinned up at her. 'Food smells that bad, does it, love?'

'Don't you start, Archie,' she said. She put the plates down. Boiled white fish, liquid mashed potatoes and carrots that had been sliced but not peeled.

'Could I see the wine list?' asked Archie. He couldn't see her mouth behind her mask but he could tell from her eyes that she was smiling.

'You're a terrible man, Archie,' she said, shaking her head as she walked away, swinging the tray.

Charlie was already tucking into his meal.

'So what was your favourite movie about serial killers, Archie?' asked Billy.

'American Psycho was a laugh,' said Archie. 'But it was more like a cartoon, not real at all. The best one, I think, is Mr Brooks.'

'Mr Brooks?' said Billy. 'I don't think I know that one.'

'It's a Kevin Costner movie. He's a serial killer who's never been caught. He has these conversations with this other guy but this other guy is really his conscience or alter ego or something.'

'Like Dexter's "dark passenger" you mean?' said Charlie.

'Yeah, sort of. Costner gets blackmailed into taking on a protege and he has to find a way of saving his skin.'

'Dexter's brilliant,' said Billy. 'But the best movie has to be Silence Of The Lambs.'

Archie nodded his approval. 'It rubs the lotion on its skin or else it gets the hose again.' He shuddered with pleasure at the words.

Charlie waved his knife at them. 'That's the one thing I didn't like about that movie. The whole skin thing. Who kills for the skin?'

Archie nodded. 'True.'

'You kill for the fun of it. For the experience. The kill is an end in itself.'

Archie nodded even more enthusiastically.

A clattering sound behind them made them jump and they turned to see the one-legged man in a wheelchair staring down at his knife on the floor. Archie got up and went over to an empty table, picked up a clean knife and took it over to the man. 'There you go, mate,' said Archie.

The man took it with a shaking hand. 'Thanks, Bob,' he said.

'I'm Archie.'

'Archie?'

'Yeah. Archie.' Archie patted him on the shoulder. 'Take it easy, mate.'

The man looked at Archie with watery eyes. 'They took my medals.'

'Your medals?'

The man nodded. 'Yeah. I'm a hero. I met the Queen.'

Archie smiled. 'That's nice.' He patted the man on the shoulder again then went back to sit at his table.

'Introducing yourself to Sergeant Caplan?' said Charlie.

Archie picked up his fork. 'Was he a cop?'

Charlie shook his head. 'Paratrooper. He was injured in the Falklands.'

'He thought I was someone called Bob.'

'Yeah. Bob's his son. He's in America now. Came to say goodbye about two years ago but Melvyn doesn't remember.' He tapped the side of his head. 'Dementia or Alzheimer's. One or the other.'

'Or both,' said Billy.

'That's a bugger,' said Archie. 'You live your life and then you forget everything.'

'And then you die,' said Billy.

'Bloody hell, will you two cheer up,' said Archie. He reached into his pocket and brought out a small bottle of whisky. He looked around and then poured some into his cup.

Charlie and Billy looked at him in amazement. Archie grinned and held up the bottle. 'Want some?'

'Hell yeah,' said Charlie. Archie checked to make sure no one was looking and poured whisky into their cups. They both sipped it appreciatively.

'It never goes away, does it?' said Charlie. 'The urge.'

'For what?' said Archie.

Charlie lowered his voice. 'For killing.'

Archie and Billy nodded in agreement.

'It's like an itch that I can't scratch,' said Billy.

Archie nodded. 'There's not a day goes by when I don't miss it.'

'Crave it,' said Charlie.

All three men nod in agreement.

'When was the first time you knew you'd have to stop?' asked Billy.

Archie held up his hands. 'I couldn't do it. I had my hands around her neck and I squeezed and nothing happened. I was... weak. I couldn't exert enough pressure. My hands were fucked.'

'So what did you do?' asked Billy.

'I had a knife. I managed to do a few more over the next year or so, but... I just got too old, you know?'

'Yeah, I know,' said Billy. He sipped his whisky-spiked tea. 'Getting old sucks. When I was younger I was good-looking, I was fit, I could talk the birds down from the trees. Getting girls was easy. Once I got older and put on a bit of weight, it got harder. I needed to carry a knife to make them do what I wanted. It did get easier when I hit sixty because they never think a grandad is going to kill them. But the problem then was it got harder to control them. I knew my days were numbered when I grabbed a girl and she hit me so hard I was seeing stars. Then she ran and I went after her. I couldn't catch her. I was fucked. Then a few years after that I got arthritis in my knees and that's when I retired.'

Charlie nodded. 'Knees and backs, they only get worse as you get older.' He held up his hands and the two men could see the slight tremble. 'I started to get the shakes. Couldn't tie knots, couldn't put gags on, couldn't pick locks. It got ridiculous.'

They finished their lunch and went through to the day room. The television was on but the sound was muted. They sat at the window table and Billy opened his box of dominoes and spread them out. 'You guys never get bored with this?' asked Archie.

'What's the alternative?' asked Charlie.

'I dunno. I was a big fan of the old horses,' said Archie. 'We could go down the bookies.'

'I'm skint,' said Charlie. 'I don't have money to throw away at a bookies.'

'If you study the form it's an investment.'

'Pull the other one,' said Charlie. 'Gambling is a mug's game. Anyway, like I said, I don't have money to waste on gambling.'

'Cards then,' said Archie. 'We don't have to play for money, we can play for points, same as we're doing now.'

'What sort of cards?' asked Billy. 'We'd need four for bridge and I don't see anyone here who'd be up for it.'

'Poker,' said Archie.

'Ah, poker,' said Charlie. 'That's not a bad idea. I used to play, back in the day. Five card stud was my favourite.'

'Were you any good?' asked Archie.

'I did okay,' said Charlie. 'I was pretty good at reading people.' He grinned. 'And I was a good liar, too. I could bluff until the cows came home.'

They heard a noise at the door and all turned to look. Mrs Woodhouse was with a man in his thirties who was wearing a Victorian frock coat and a top hat and carrying a large leather Gladstone bag. 'Fuck me,' said Archie. 'That's either an undertaker or Jack The Ripper.'

Charlie chuckled. 'He's a wannabe magician. The Great Spiro or Spigot or something. He comes in every few weeks to entertain the residents, though entertain is stretching it a bit.'

Mrs Woodhouse took the man over to the television. She switched it off, clapped her hands and announced that the residents were in for a treat. Only a handful of the residents paid her any attention, though a little old lady sitting on a sofa in front of the television giggled and clapped as enthusiastically as a toddler.

Mrs Woodhouse left the room as the magician made spindle legs appear from the bag. He placed it on the floor, opened it and took out a magic wand He tapped the wand against the bag and it turned into a bunch of flowers. The little old lady gasped and clapped. Most of the residents weren't paying attention and the few that were looking in his direction had blank eyes and open mouths.

The magician popped the flowers into the bag and took out three large stainless steel rings which he proceeded to push together and pull apart in a variety of ways, all of which seemed to entrance the little old lady.

Archie wasn't sure whether he should feel pity or scorn for the magician. The tricks weren't great and he clearly had no talent, but on the other hand the man was giving up his time to entertain folks who generally only had the television for company.

Charlie clearly had no difficulty deciding how to react. He cupped his hands around his mouth and shouted over at him. 'Hey, David Copperfield, can you make yourself disappear?'

The magician's cheeks reddened but he ignored the outburst.

73

'What card am I thinking of?' shouted Charlie. 'I'll give you a hint. It's the Queen of fuck off out of here.'

Charlie laughed and sat back in his chair. 'That's a bit harsh, mate,' said Archie. 'The guy's doing his best.'

An old man with a straggly white beard let out a howl. Everton rushed over to see what was wrong, and when the care worker helped him to his feet they could see that he'd wet himself. The magician turned a line of white handkerchiefs red and blue as Everton helped the man to the bathroom.

'Come on, let's get out of here,' said Archie.

Charlie looked up from the dominoes. 'Hey, come on, I'm winning,' he said.

'I need some fresh air,' said Archie.

CHAPTER 15

They took the mobility scooters and drove to the promenade and parked so that they could overlook the beach. The tide was out and there was almost five hundred metres of pristine sand between the promenade and the sea. The sky overhead was a cloudless blue but a chill wind blew off the sea and they were all wearing coats and scarfs. Off to their right was the Eiffel Tower copy that had been dominating the Blackpool skyline since 1894.

Archie slid the bottle of whisky from his coat, took a sip, and waved the bottle at the tower in the distance. 'Did you know that when that was built it was the tallest man-made structure in the British Empire?'

'I did not know that,' said Billy, holding out his hand. Archie laughed and gave him the bottle. 'But there's bugger all of an empire left these days.'

'No one gives a fuck about us,' said Charlie. 'But if you grab a rubber dingy and sail over from France, they'll put you up in a four star hotel and let you bring your whole fucking family in. This country has gone to the dogs.'

Billy took a long gulp of whisky, then gave the bottle back to Archie who passed it on to Charlie. Charlie gulped down some whisky, then waved the bottle at the sea. 'No one gives a shit about the likes of us. Do you know many old folk died in care homes in England? Thirty-five fucking thousand. Do you know how many asylum seekers died of it? Not one. Not a single fucking one.' He waved his bottle at the sea. 'It's no wonder they keep coming. We're the softest touch in the world.'

Archie laughed. 'Well one thing's for sure, they're not coming that way,' he said. 'That's the Irish Sea. The Channel is behind us.'

'You know what I mean,' said Charlie. He took another long pull on the whisky and gave it back to Archie. 'During lockdown we weren't allowed to leave the building. Couldn't go to doctors appointments, couldn't even go for a walk in the garden. Total lockdown. But those ISIS bastards just kept on coming and they were welcomed with open arms. Driven to posh hotels in fucking limousines, and not a mask to be seen. They took a group of them on a day trip to Anfield. It was in the papers. All these Asian fuckers in designer gear with state of the art mobiles being shown around the Liverpool ground, and I wasn't even allowed to visit the shops.' He shook his head in disgust. 'The previous manager wanted us all to clap for the NHS and I told him to go shove his claps where the sun don't shine. The NHS did nothing for me. The government did even less. They want me dead and that's the end of it.'

'Fucking hell mate, calm down,' said Archie. 'Did you take your blood pressure medication today?'

Charlie chuckled. 'I did, squire, thanks for asking.'

They heard a child cry off to the left and they all turned to look to see where the noise was coming from. Down on the beach, a mother and father were trying to get their young son to sit on a donkey. The boy clearly didn't want to do it and the father began to shout at him.

'Parents, huh?' said Charlie. 'Why would they force him to do something he doesn't what to do?'

'They want him to have fun,' said Archie.

'Does that look like fun?' asked Charlie. 'Riding a flea-bitten nag on a freezing cold beach?'

Archie laughed and gave him the bottle. 'Have another drink, mate,' he said. 'Sounds like you need it.'

Charlie grunted and drank. A double-decker cream and green Heritage tram rattled by, filled with holidaymakers bundled up in warm clothing and wearing covid masks.

'Let's change the subject,' said Archie. 'Who would your ideal be?'

Charlie frowned. 'Ideal?'

'Ideal victim. You know, in a perfect world, if you could do anyone, who would you do?'

'Grace Kelly,' said Billy quickly. 'She was my ideal. I saw her in a Hitchcock movie when I was a kid and it was like I spent my whole life looking for someone like her.'

Archie nodded. 'She was beautiful. No question. Yeah, I'd have done Grace Kelly.'

Charlie took another swig from the bottle then wiped his mouth with his sleeve. 'Halle Berry,' he said.

'Good call,' said Archie. 'Beautiful girl.'

'God no,' said Billy. 'I hate black skin.'

Charlie looked over at him. 'Racist.'

'That's not racist,' said Billy. 'I mean I hate the colour. You can't see the blood.'

Charlie squinted at him. 'What do you mean, you can't see the blood?'

Billy sighed. 'Red on black. There's no contrast. It just looks wet. Now you cut a blonde with alabaster white skin, then you can really see the blood.'

Archie grinned at Charlie. 'He's got a point.' He took out his cigarettes and lit one. He saw Billy looking enviously at the pack so offered one to him. Billy took it and Archie lit it for him.

'So I'm an idiot for liking black birds?' said Charlie.

Billy sighed. 'I'm not saying you're an idiot. I'm just saying that for aesthetic reasons, I prefer white skin.'

'The world would be a very boring place if we all liked the same thing,' said Archie.

Charlie nodded. 'True that.' He took another drink from the bottle. 'Kate Middleton.'

He passed the bottle back to Archie. 'What? The Queen? That's out of order, mate. That's out of order.'

'She's not the Queen yet.'

'Even so... It's out of order. You don't fuck with the Royal Family.'

'What about Diana?'

'What about Diana? That was an accident. The driver was drunk.'

'No, I mean, would you have done Diana?'

Archie glared at him. 'What the fuck is wrong with you? I said no Royal Family.'

Charlie held up his hands. 'Okay. Okay.'

'Debbie Harry,' said Billy. 'Back in the Eighties I spent months looking for a girl who looked like her. Found a couple but never got the opportunity.'

'The Blondie singer?' said Archie. 'Yes, definitely. I always liked them small.'

'And Patsy Kensit. She was in that movie with David Bowie.'

'Absolute Beginners. Yeah.' Archie grinned. 'She was fit back then. Not so fit when she was in Eastenders. Put on a bit of weight, she did. And too much plastic surgery.' He nodded at Billy. 'You really do have a thing for blondes.'

'Can't deny it,' said Billy.

'You only ever did blondes?'

Billy nodded. 'It was my thing. Brunettes and redheads never did it for me. There's just something about blonde hair.'

'Was your mum blonde?' asked Archie.

Billy's face darkened and he pointed a finger at Archie. 'Don't fucking try to analyse me,' he said.

'What?'

'You're saying that it's because of my mum that I turned out the way I am.'

'Fuck me, mate, I was just having a conversation.'

'About my mum?'

'Mate, you keep saying you have a thing about blondes.'

'Yeah, I do., But that's got nothing to do with my mum.'

'Fine. So she was what? Chinese?'

'No she was blonde. Happy now?'

'It's not about me being happy,' said Archie. 'I just wondered.'

'I don't hate women,' said Billy.

'No one said you did.'

'No, you inferred that my mum did something bad to me and that because of that I started killing blonde women.'

'Implied,' said Charlie.

'What?'

'Implied. Not inferred. When you say something but mean something else, that's implying. But if you read something into something Archie said, that's inferring. Now Archie wasn't implying that your mum is who started you killing, but you inferred that.'

'What the fuck are you talking about, Charlie?'

Archie waved his hand dismissively. 'It doesn't matter. Seriously, mate, I wasn't implying anything. I was just making conversation.'

'Anyway, she left when I was eight,' said Billy. 'Packed her bags and left without a by your leave.' He shrugged. 'Dad said she'd run off with another man.'

'Did you believe him?' asked Archie.

'Now what are you implying?' He said. 'I'm using the right word this time, right?'

'I'm not implying anything,' said Archie. 'I'm just curious. I ask a lot of questions. It's my thing.' He shrugged. 'What can I say, I'm interested in people.'

'Yeah, well you should remember that curiosity killed the cat.'

Archie studied Billy as he took a long drag on his cigarette and then blew smoke towards the beach. 'You wouldn't be threatening me, would you Billy?' he asked.

'Will the two of you stop with the chest-beating,' said Charlie. 'What's it going to be, colostomy bags at dawn?'

Archie laughed. 'Yeah, you're right. Sorry, Billy. I've no business prying into your personal life.' He flicked away the remains of his cigarette. 'Come on, I need to buy some more fags and booze. And teabags.'

He switched on the scooter and headed down the promenade. Charlie and Billy followed.

They crossed the promenade and headed to the road that ran parallel to it. It was a different world. The main beach road was lined with hotels, restaurants, gift shops and amusement arcades, but one street away there were weeds growing up through the pavements, litter gathering in the gutters and houses that didn't appear to have been painted in decades. Despite the thousands of tourists who flocked to the town every day, Blackpool was consistently rated one of the most deprived areas of the United Kingdom, with a growing drug problem and the highest unemployment rate in the country.

Two young men in hoodies sharing a roll-up watched the three men go by. 'Put your foot down, grandad!' one of them shouted. 'Let's see you pull a doughnut!'

'Get a job!' shouted Charlie.

The two men laughed. One of them picked up an empty lager can and threw it. It bounced off the back of Billy's scooter and clattered onto the pavement.

'Wankers,' shouted Billy.

They reached a line of shops - an off licence, a newsagents, a hairdressers and an electrical shop. Archie parked outside the off-licence and went inside while Charlie and Billy cruised past the rest of the shops.

A hairdresser was blow-drying a customer's hair, wearing a full plastic face mask and blue latex gloves. Another customer was waiting to be served, a cloth face mask covering her mouth but not her nose. She was in her late twenties with shoulder length hair. Billy smiled at her. She looked back at him and nodded. Billy waved and her eyes sparkled.

'Stop that,' hissed Charlie.

'Stop what?' said Billy. 'I'm just being polite.'

'I know what you're thinking.'

Billy chuckled. 'A man can dream, can't he?'

They pulled up outside the electrical shop. A sign across the top of the window announced a closing-down sale but it had clearly been there for a long time as it had faded in the sun. There were half a dozen laptops in the window, along with a display of CCTV cameras and smoke and fire detectors. A brown teddy bear was sitting on a small chair next to a sign that read - NANNY CAM - KEEP YOUR CHILDREN SAFE. Charlie tilted his head on one side as he looked at the bear, then he climbed off his scooter. 'Give me a minute,' he said.

As he disappeared inside the shop, a teenage girl in a pink tracksuit crossed the road. At a distance she looked like a teenager but as she got closer Billy could see that she was in her thirties. Her skin was dry and flaking and pockmarked with old acne scars. She rubbed her nose with the back of her hand and he caught a glimpse of dirty fingernails bitten to the quick. 'Got any spare change, mister?' She whined.

'I'm skint, love,' said Billy.

She rubbed her nose again as she looked at Charlie's scooter.

'Don't even think about it,' he said.

'What?'

'Pinching my friend's scooter,' said Billy. 'It's not the greatest getaway vehicle and you'd have trouble selling it.'

She sniffed. 'I wasn't thinking about stealing it.'

'Yes you were.'

She wiped her nose with her sleeve again. 'Wasn't.'

Archie rolled up on his scooter and parked next to Billy. He had put a bottle wrapped in white paper in the front basket along with a carrier bag. 'What's happening?' he asked.

'She's thinking about pinching Archie's scooter.'

'I wasn't,' said the girl, shifting her weight from foot to foot. 'Why do you keep saying that?'

Archie looked around. 'Where is Charlie?'

Billy gestured at the shop behind them. 'He went in there.'

'Have you got any spare change?' asked the girl.

Archie tilted his head on one side as he looked at her. 'What's your name, love?'

'Sarah,' she said. 'But they call me Scraps.

'Why do they call you Scraps?'

She shrugged and wiped her nose again. 'I dunno. They just do.'

'What are you on, Scraps? Heroin? Meth? Skunk? Spice?'

She narrowed her eyes. 'What you got?'

Archie laughed and waved away her question. 'I'm not a dealer, Scraps. I was just curious.'

'What's spice?' asked Billy.

'It's synthetic cannabis,' said Archie.

'It's wicked,' said Scraps. 'You got any?'

Archie laughed again and pointed at the wrapped-up bottle in his basket. 'Alcohol has always been my drug of choice,' he said. 'Alcohol and cigarettes.'

'Booze is a killer,' she said. 'My dad was an alkie. Booze killed him.'

'Everything in moderation,' said Billy.

'Where are you from, Scraps?' asked Archie.

Her face hardened. 'What are you, social services?'

'Sorry, love, I just like to ask questions. It's my thing.'

'I can vouch for that,' said Billy. 'He does like asking questions.'

'You're a nosy fucker?'

Archie laughed. 'I guess you could say that. But you don't sound like you're from around here. East London, maybe. Or Essex.'

She nodded. 'London. Islington.'

'So what are you doing here in sunny Blackpool?

'The social sent me. Said I had more chance of getting work here but that was a lie, they just didn't want to pay London prices for accommodation. And as soon as I did move they cut my money anyway. Bastards.'

'So where do you stay?

She pointed to the left. 'I've got a bedsit over there. It's a shithole.'

'And no luck getting a job?'

She snorted with derision. 'Do you have any idea what the odds of getting a job are in Blackpool? It's not just an unemployment blackspot, it's a black fucking hole.'

'If you don't mind me asking, how old are you, love?'

'Fuck me you do like asking questions, don't you?'

Archie shrugged. 'I'm sorry.'

'I'm twenty-four.' She sneered at him. 'You're going to tell me I look older, aren't you?'

Archie shook his head. 'I'd never say that to a lady,' he said. In fact that was exactly what he had been thinking,. He'd have guessed her age at mid-thirties. Clearly whatever drugs she was using were taking their toll.

'Lady!' she laughed. 'It's a long time since I was called that.' She smiled showing yellowed teeth and brushed a lock of her lank hair behind her ear. 'What's your name?' she asked.

'Archie.'

She leaned towards him. 'Archie, have you got any spare change on you?'

Archie laughed. 'I don't think anyone has any spare change these days.' Her face fell but then brightened when he reached for his wallet. He took out a twenty pound note but when she held out her hand he pulled it away. 'Promise me one thing, love.'

'What? Yes. Sure. What?'

'Don't spend it on drugs. Get yourself some food or soap or shampoo or put it towards your electricity bill.'

She nodded furiously. 'Sure. Yes, No problem.' He gave her the note and she grabbed it, then hurried away as if she was afraid he would change his mind. As she reached a side road she turned and gave him the finger. 'Wanker!' she shouted.

Archie chuckled as she disappeared around the corner. Charlie came out of the shop carrying a box. 'What was that about?' he asked, putting the box into the basket on the front of the scooter.

'Archie just gave a junkie twenty quid,' said Billy.

'If you want to throw money away, squire, throw it in my direction,' said Charlie, climbing on to the seat of his scooter.

'I was just trying to help the girl,' said Archie. He lit a cigarette. 'Her life is a mess.'

'No one is forcing her to be a junkie,' said Billy.

Archie blew smoke at the road. 'It's an illness. Like she said, her dad was an alcoholic, and that's an illness too. My dad was a drinker. He'd drink until he passed out. Didn't matter how much my mum complained, didn't matter how much his kids begged him not to drink, he still drank.'

'People make their own decisions,' said Charlie. 'Sometimes they make good decisions, sometimes they make bad decisions, but at the end of the day people get the lives they choose.'

Billy was looking longingly at Archie's cigarette so he gave him the pack and the lighter. 'Okay, Charlie, answer me this then. Your life, the life you had, and by that I mean the real life, the life you've had to keep secret all these years, how much of that was a choice?'

Billy finished lighting his cigarette and passed the pack and the lighter back to Archie.

'What are you saying, that I'm sick?' asked Charlie.

Archie put the pack and lighter away. 'Did you make a conscious decision to become a serial killer, that's the question I'm asking.' He waved at Billy. 'Did any of us? Was it a career choice?'

Charlie frowned. 'I killed because I liked it. It was the biggest rush, ever.'

Billy nodded. 'Nothing comes close. It's better than any drug.'

'It's better than a drug because it is a drug,' said Archie. 'Killing is an addiction. Every time you do it your brain gets an endorphin rush and that's why killers become serial killers, they want to recapture that rush. And that's no different to being an alcoholic or a drug addict.'

'So you're saying we're addicts?'

'You tell me. I asked you, was it a career choice? Did you decide one day to go out and kill? Or was it a burning desire that grew and grew until you couldn't fight it any longer?'

'That's what it was like for me,' said Billy. 'It was a need. I had to do it. I had no choice.'

'Exactly,' said Archie.

'So you're saying that we're the same as a fucking junkie?' sneered Charlie.

'I'm saying that sometimes we're driven by impulses rather than decisions, and if I want to give a few quid to a woman who's been dealt a shit hand, then that's my call. Billy here says she chose to be a junkie, but maybe not, maybe it's in her DNA. And maybe we're the way we are because of our DNA.'

'So now you're a psychiatrist?' said Charlie.

'I'm just a student of human nature,' he said. He flicked ash onto the pavement. 'I spend a lot of time thinking about the way I turned out. How much of the man I've become is because of my genes, and how much because of the way I was brought up.'

'Nature or nurture?' said Charlie.

'Exactly. Coupled with the decisions I've made in my life. It's funny when you think about it, but with all the randomness in our lives, the three of us end up in the same place.'

'Birds of a feather,' said Billy.

'Yeah, birds of a fucking feather,' said Archie. He looked at his watch. 'Time to go.'

They drove in single file along the pavement, Archie leading the way, Billy following and Charlie bringing up the rear.

Ahead of them two teenagers with shaved heads, bomber jackets and tight jeans with black Doc Marten boots were walking towards him with a massive brown pit bull between them. Archie slowed and moved to the edge of the pavement to give them plenty of room as he went by, but even so the dog was spooked and began barking and snapping.

The barking increased as Archie drove by and he took a quick look over his shoulder. The dog was straining at the leash and snapping at Billy. The two skinheads began shouting abuse at Billy and he ducked as one of them lashed out, trying to slap the back of his head.

'Get off the pavement you fucking wanker!' shouted the man holding the leash.

Billy accelerated away. The two men turned to face Charlie, who had slowed to a crawl. The dog was barking crazily, up on its back legs as its owner tried to pull him back.

'Steady guys!' shouted Charlie. He tried to ease past them but there was barely any room between the snarling dog and the edge of the pavement. 'Let me get by, why don't you?'

The dog lunged forward and Charlie jerked the handlebars to get away but then he had to brake to avoid falling into the road. The two skinheads continued to shout and swear at him, then one of them kicked the rear of the scooter, hard enough to move it a few inches. The other skinhead put his foot against the front of the scooter and they both pushed.

Archie brought his scooter to a halt. 'Hey, come on, don't be pricks!' he shouted. He climbed off his scooter but as his feet touched the pavement the skinheads pushed Charlie into the road. The scooter keeled over and crashed onto the tarmac. Charlie rolled into the road and the scooter fell on top of him. He screamed in pain and the skinheads laughed as the dog continued to bark.

'Fucking wanker!' shouted one.

The other cleared his throat and spat at Charlie but the phlegm missed and splattered over the scooter. The men laughed and headed up the promenade, the dog still snarling and barking.

Archie hurried over to Charlie. The scooter was on his leg and Archie tried to lift it off him, but he didn't have the strength. Billy parked his scooter and hurried over. He joined Archie and together the two of them managed to lift the scooter enough so that Charlie could pull his leg free.

'Bastards,' muttered Charlie. 'They could've fucking killed me.'

'How's the leg?' asked Archie.

Charlie rubbed it. 'It's okay. Not broken.'

Archie helped Charlie to his feet. 'You're sure?'

Charlie tested the leg and nodded. 'I'm okay. Could've been worse.'

Archie and Billy grabbed the scooter and tried to push it upright but it was just too heavy. Billy groaned and they lowered it back to the ground.

They tried again but still couldn't get it upright, then Charlie seized the rear of the scooter and together they managed to get it upright and then they lifted it back onto the pavement. Archie checked it over but despite a few scratches on the side that had hit the road, there didn't seem to be any damage. Billy picked up the box and gave it to Charlie. 'What's that then?'

'Just a present for Mrs Chalmers,' said Charlie. He put the box in the scooter's front carrier and climbed on. 'Come on, last one back at the ranch is a wanker,' he said, and sped off.

CHAPTER 16

Everton carried three plates over to their table, one in each hand and one on his left arm. 'That's a very professional move there, mate,' said Archie. 'You worked in a restaurant?'

'Two years at the Mana,' he said as he put the plates down in front of them.

'You are pulling my leg,' said Archie.

'No, I did three years there.'

'What's the Mana?' asked Billy.

'It's the only restaurant in Manchester that has a Michelin star,' said Archie.

'To be fair, they got the star a few months after I left,' said Everton.

'Maybe that was why,' said Charlie, with a sly grin.

'You've heard of it, right?' asked Archie. Charlie shook his head. 'A chef called Simon Martin opened it and got his star after a year. He worked with Gordon Ramsay in London.' He looked up at Everton. 'You worked with Martin, right?'

'Only for a few months. Guy's a genius but he works his people hard. I couldn't be bothered with it, but I learnt a lot, that's for sure.'

'Doesn't he do a tasting menu with eighteen items on it?'

Everton laughed. 'Nineteen. Nineteen courses.'

'Who can eat nineteen courses?' asked Charlie.

'Most of them are really small,' said Everton.

'And what would it cost, a meal like that?' asked Billy.

'An arm and a leg,' said Everton. He gave them a mock bow. 'Enjoy your meal, gentlemen,' he said.

Archie looked down at his plate as Everton walked away. A pale chicken breast sat in a pool of white liquid next to half a dozen slices of carrots and a couple of spoonfuls of curly pasta. He shook his head sadly. 'They feed prisoners better than this.'

'They get a choice, too, in prison,' said Charlie.

'Have you been inside?' asked Archie. He cut off a small piece of chicken and chewed it, It was flavourless and rubbery.

'Nah, but I've got mates who did time.' He laughed. 'They're both dead now. But they said that they got three meals a day and for lunch and tea they had a choice of five meals.'

'Five?' repeated Billy.

'Yeah. There's regular, vegetarian, low-fat, halal, and something else. It wasn't great food, they said, but at least they had a choice.'

They ate in silence for a while. A woman began to sob in the far corner of the dining room and Sally hurried over to the table to see what was wrong. Charlie waved his knife in the crying woman's direction. 'Another one of Connolly's victims,' he said. He sighed and cut off a chunk of chicken. 'We could do it, if we worked together,' he said quietly.

'Do what?' asked Billy.

'You know what,' said Charlie. 'Do what we do. What we all want to do. What we need to do.'

'You're crazy,' Billy laughed.

'Yeah, well we're all crazy,' said Archie.

Charlie shook his head. 'We're not crazy. We're different. But crazy or not crazy isn't the point. The point is, working together. We're stronger. Together we could scratch our itch.'

Archie's eyes narrowed. 'Are you serious?' He looked over at Billy. 'Is he fucking serious?"

'As cancer,' said Charlie. 'No offence, Archie.'

Archie nodded. 'None taken.'

Charlie leaned forward and lowered his voice. 'It was when that scooter fell onto the road that I realised. One of us couldn't lift it back onto the pavement. Nor could two of us.' He grinned. 'But the three of us, working together...'

Billy was still toying with his food. 'We could kill the chef,' he said.

Archie and Charlie laughed. Billy looked up from his plate. 'I'm serious.'

'Mate, this isn't the best place to be having a conversation about murdering the cook,' said Archie. He gestured with his knife at Connolly, who was sitting at a table with Mrs Chalmers, holding a spoonful of pasta just out of reach of her mouth and whispering to her. Tears were running down her face.

They finished their food and went out into the garden. The sky was darkening but it didn't look like rain. They went over to a bench. Tape had been stuck across the bench to demonstrate that only two people should sit there, but they ignored it and sat together, Archie in the middle.

Archie took out his cigarettes, then lit one for himself and for Billy. He saw Charlie looking wistfully at the packet and offered it to him. 'I've given up,' said Charlie. 'I told you that.'

Archie grinned, 'One won't kill you.'

'Get thee behind me, Satan,' said Charlie. Then he laughed and reached for the pack. 'Fuck it, no one lives forever, right?' He took out a cigarette and Archie lit it for him. 'You're a dangerous man, Archie,' he said, before putting it between his lips and taking a long drag.

'Strictly speaking, we all are,' said Archie.

Charlie held the smoke in his lungs for several seconds, then slowly blew a tight plume down at the grass. 'God, I've missed that,' he said.

Billy tried to blow a smoke ring but failed miserably.

Archie chuckled. 'Watch this,' he said. He took a pull on his cigarette and blew an almost perfect circle of smoke. As it grew he blew a second ring through the first.

'Show off,' said Charlie.

'Practice makes perfect,' said Archie.

Charlie tried to blow a smoke ring but was even less successful than Billy had been. Billy tried again but then broke into a fit of coughing. Archie patted him on the knee. 'Careful, mate.'

Billy nodded, took a deep breath, and nodded. 'I'm okay,' he said.

They sat in silence for a while, blowing smoke rings up at the clouds above. It was Archie who spoke first. 'What was it like, Charlie? Your first time?'

Charlie flicked ash onto the grass. 'My first time? It was an accident, really.'

'An accident?'

Charlie leaned back and looked up at the sky. 'There was a quarry near where we lived. We'd swim there in the summer. All the local kids went. One day I was there with a younger kid. A girl. Just the two of us. I dunno how that happened. She was walking a dog, I think. The dog had run off and I said I'd help her. We were talking and she said she couldn't swim. I just kept getting the urge to push her in and watch her drown. So I did.' He shrugged and took a pull on his cigarette and blew smoke before continuing. 'It felt so fucking good. Seeing the look of panic in her eyes. And watching her go under.' Charlie shuddered with pleasure at the memory, then he turned to look at Archie. 'What about you? What was your first time like?'

'Me? Ah, that was a hooker. I never knew her name. It was in Salford, I was thirty-six. I was a bit drunk. She was rat-arsed. She said I could fuck her for a fiver and I had a fiver so we went down an alley and I fucked her. Then she started crying rape and that I should give her fifty quid and the only way I could shut her up was to put my hands around her throat. I squeezed and I watched the life fade from her eyes.'

'You used a condom, right?'

'She was a hooker, of course I used a condom.'

'I meant DNA. You don't want to be leaving DNA behind.'

'I know, I know. Anyway, I left her in the alley and ran. For the next week or so I jumped at every knock on the door, I was sure the cops would come for me. But they never did and after a while I started

91

to crave it. I wanted to do it again. So I did, but I put more planning into the second one.' He blew smoke up at the sky. 'God, I miss it.'

'Me too,' said Billy.

'We all do,' said Charlie. 'That's why we should give it a go. Do something together, as a team.'

'A last hurrah?' said Archie.

'If we did it. How would we…you know, get it done?' asked Billy.

'Same as we used to,' said Archie. 'SSS.'

Billy frowned. 'SSS?'

'It's a mnemonic. Select, Stalk, Strike.'

Charlie chuckled. 'Choose. Catch. Kill. That was mine.'

'Three Cs?' said Billy.

Charlie laughed. 'Close. What about you?''

'I never made lists,' said Billy. 'I just did it.'

Charlie frowned. 'You didn't plan?'

'I planned. Of course I planned. But I didn't have a set plan. I just did whatever I had to do. Horses for courses.'

'The point is we need to select a victim,' said Charlie. 'Then work out how we can do the kill.'

'And we'd have to dispose of the body,' said Billy. 'That's always the hard bit.'

'We can do it,' said Charlie. 'I know we can do it.'

Connolly pushed a woman in a wheelchair down the ramp from the back door. He was wearing full PPE, a plastic suit, an N95 mask and a plastic face guard, but once outside he flicked up the face guard and pulled off the mask so that it hung around his neck. He pushed the wheelchair to a bench at the far side of the garden and sat down. The three men watched as Connolly took a tobacco pouch from his pocket and rolled a cigarette. He lit it, then blew smoke straight into the face of the old lady.

'We could do him,' said Billy. 'I'd love to stick a knife in his throat and watch him bleed.'

Charlie shook his head. 'No, no, no.'

'Why not? The bastard deserves it.'

Charlie sighed. 'What's the first rule of being a serial killer? Come on. What's the first rule?'

Billy frowned. 'Don't talk about serial killing?'

'That's Fight Club, you twat. The first rule about serial killing is that you never, ever, kill someone you know.'

Archie nodded in agreement. 'That's amateur hour.'

'Like Fred West,' said Charlie. 'He killed people he knew.'

'And buried the bodies under his house,' said Archie.

'Amateur. If we kill Connolly, the first thing the cops will do is to see who wanted him dead.'

'It'll be a long bloody list,' said Billy.

'Yeah, but there'll be a list,' said Charlie. 'And we'll be on it. I don't want to get caught.'

'If we do this right, we won't get caught,' said Billy. He looked over at Connolly. He was leaning towards the old lady and blowing smoke straight into her eyes as tears ran down her wrinkled cheeks. Billy's jaw tightened as he glared at Connolly with undisguised hatred.

Charlie patted him on the leg. 'Easy, tiger,' he said. 'Step by step. Remember the six Ps. Perfect Planning Prevents Piss-Poor Performance.'

Billy smiled thinly but his eyes stayed fixed on Connolly. 'Okay, mate, I hear you.'

CHAPTER 17

Charlie woke up at seven-thirty as dawn broke. He never needed an alarm, he was always wide awake the moment the sun's rays shone through the threadbare curtains. He sat up and swung his feet over the edge of the bed, then waited a few seconds before standing up. He padded over to the bathroom. He used an electric razor to shave because his trembling hands meant that even a safety razor caused havoc to his skin. He showered and dried himself, then went back into his tiny bedroom and took a pair of Y-fronts and socks from the top drawer of the chest of drawers. He leaned against it as he slowly put his right leg into the Y-fronts and pulled them up to his knees, then he repeated the process with his left leg. Once he'd pulled the Y-fronts all the way up he sat down and began the long process of putting on his socks. His bad back and belly fat meant that he couldn't bend forward enough to slip the socks on, instead he had to toss the sock forward and hope that he could get his toes into it, then pull it up the foot. It took him half a dozen tries to get the first one on, and by the time he had done both he was red faced and out of breath. He sat and took several deep breaths before standing up and walking over to the Victorian wardrobe where he kept his few clothes. He took a pair of grey trousers off a wire hanger and used the same technique as he'd used with his underwear, right leg and then left leg as he leaned against the wardrobe for balance. He was down to his last clean shirt as the home only did laundry once a week. It was long sleeved which he hated because it was such a pain fastening the buttons on the cuffs, but he pulled it on and stood in front of the wardrobe mirror as he slowly buttoned it up.

It was half past eight by the time he had dressed. He slipped on a pair of tartan slippers, picked up his walking stick and left his room. He walked down the corridor to the room where Mrs Chalmers slept. The old lady was almost deaf so there was no point in knocking. He opened the door and slipped inside.

She was snoring softly, her mouth wide open. Her wig was on the bedside table, along with a glass containing her dentures. One of the care-workers would come to wake, bathe and dress her at nine, so he knew he had plenty of time.

The room was identical to his own, though there were more personal items. There were framed photographs on one wall of her and her family. One was a wedding photograph that must have been taken seventy years earlier. She was stunning back then, tall and willowy with long black hair, high cheekbones and sparkling eyes, holding the arm of a man in an officer's uniform. There were photographs of her with the same man, one taken in front of the Taj Mahal, and then others of them with children, eventually three, two girls and a boy. In the most recent photographs she was in her fifties, and still a good looking lady. It was hard to reconcile the beautiful woman in the pictures with the wizened husk of a human being lying in the bed. In all the time that Charlie had been at the home, he'd never seen her with a visitor. Her family had either passed away or abandoned her.

A line of old soft toys had been placed on the top of the chest of drawers. A rabbit, a golliwog, a Rupert bear, three threadbare teddies, and a dog with long floppy ears. Charlie had put the Nanny-cam bear in the middle and it blended perfectly. He picked it up and rearranged the toys to fill in the gap before slipping out of the room.

As he headed down the stairs he passed Everton who was wearing full PPE and running a Hoover over the carpet. 'Morning, Charlie, bit old for a teddy bear, aren't you?' said Everton.

'Yeah, yeah, yeah,' said Charlie. He pointed at the stairs. 'You missed a bit.'

Everton grinned behind his face shield as Charlie reached the bottom of the stairs and headed down the corridor towards Mrs Woodhouse's office. Her door was closed so he knocked softly. There was no response so he knocked again, harder this time, and heard her say 'come in.'

He opened the door. Her desk was facing him and she looked up from her computer screen, clearly not happy at being interrupted, but then she forced a smile and took off her glasses. 'Yes, Charlie, how can I help you?'

'I just need a word, Mrs Woodhouse.' He closed the door behind him. To the left of the office was a long low cupboard on which stood an aquarium filled with brightly coloured fish swimming around a plastic sunken galleon and a plastic treasure chest from which bubbles cascaded. Leaning against the cupboard was her badminton bag and a pair of trainers. Mrs Woodhouse was a keen player and the regular games probably accounted for her trim figure. Charlie never had a type, but he'd always thought that if he had come across her back in his predatory days he would have enjoyed raping and killing her. 'I won't take up too much of your time,' he added.

She had placed a cup of tea next to her computer mouse, and a plate with a couple of Jaffa cakes. Charlie was a big fan of Jaffa cakes but they had never been offered to residents in all the time he had been in the home.

'That's all right, Charlie. My door is always open.'

'It wasn't though, was it?'

She frowned, not understanding what he'd said.

There were two wooden chairs facing her desk and he sat down on the one on the left. 'It was closed,' he said. 'It always is.'

A look of annoyance flashed across her face and when she smiled again he could still see the contempt in her eyes. 'Well, rhetorically it is. Most of the time.'

'Metaphorically.'

The look of annoyance was back again. 'What?''

'It's not rhetorical. The open door is a metaphor. So it's metaphorical.'

'Right..Yes. Of course.' She had spotted the bear that he was holding and was now staring at it.

Charlie waggled the bear from side to side. 'Hello Mrs Woodhouse, how are you today?' he said in a squeaky voice.

Her frown deepened. 'What?'

'We need to talk,' he said in his normal voice. 'About Connolly.'

'Jackie?'

'Jackie. He's a thief. And he's abusing the clients. Especially the female ones.'

'I'm sorry, what?'

Charlie held up the bear and did the bear voice again. 'And I've got the evidence.'

'Charlie, what are you talking about?'

He placed the bear on her desk. Then he took a USB cord from his pocket and put it down next to the bear. 'You plug one end into the bear's arse and the other end into your computer.'

She picked up the bear and looked at it. 'What's going on, Charlie?'

'It's a Nanny-cam, with a built-in memory,' he said. 'Motion and sound activated. I put it in Mrs Chalmers's room.'

'You did what?'

'The bear'll explain everything. Just plug it in.'

She frowned, then plugged the cord into the socket on the bear's behind. Then she plugged the other end into her computer. She looked on the screen.

'It should connect automatically,' he said. 'That's what it said on the booklet that came with it, though most of that was in Chinese. The diagrams were pretty self explanatory, though.'

Mrs Woodhouse put her glasses on again and peered at the screen. She clicked her mouse and moved her face closer to the computer. Charlie stood up and walked around her desk. She was so focused on the screen that she didn't seem to be aware of him coming up behind her.

The camera had been pointing towards the bed and they could clearly see Connolly walking towards the sleeping Mrs Chalmers. Charlie pointed at the time code along the bottom of the screen. 'That's two o'clock in the morning,' he said.

'I can see that,' she said frostily, peering closer at the screen.

Connolly sat down on the bed. His back was to the camera so they couldn't make out what he was doing, but it looked as if he was touching her. They could hear Mrs Chalmers begin to sob. 'See. He's assaulting her. The bastard is touching her up.'

Mrs Woodhouse frowned but didn't say anything.

'You need to call the police. You need to report him.'

Mrs Woodhouse looked closer at the screen, then sighed and sat back in her chair. She looked at him over the top of her glasses. 'All I see is Jackie comforting Mrs Chalmers. She gets confused, she has dementia and is often upset.'

'He's sitting on her bed.'

'He's trying to calm her down.'

They both looked at the screen. Mrs Chalmers was sobbing now. It looked as if Connolly was touching her chest area, but it was hard to see exactly what he was doing. But Charlie was certain of one thing - he wasn't comforting her. 'Show it to the police. Let them decide.'

She shook her head and pushed her glasses further up her nose with her finger. 'I'm not phoning the police until I've spoken to Jackie.'

'Mrs Woodhouse, he abuses half the women in here. And he steals.'

She looked at him, frowning. 'We've had no complaints of thefts.'

'Because he steals from the doolally ones.'

'Doolally?'

'The ones with dementia. The ones with Alzheimers. The ones too far gone to complain.'

'Well now you're just being ridiculous.'

Charlie shook his head, 'He's a thief, Mrs Woodhouse. And a pervert.' He pointed at the screen. 'You can see what he's doing. It's there as plain as the nose on your face.'

She flashed him a tight smile. 'I can see that Mrs Chalmers is distressed. And that Jackie is offering her comfort.'

Charlie snorted with derision. 'Between her legs? Because that's where it looks like his hand is right now.'

She looked at the screen, then took off her glasses. 'I will not have talk like that in my office.'

Charlie backed away from the desk. 'I'm sorry. But he needs to be stopped.' He walked around the desk and stood behind one of the chairs.

'Who else have you spoken to about this?'

'Nobody.'

She leaned towards him, gripping her glasses with both hands. 'Then let's keep it that way until I've had the chance to talk to Jackie.'

'You need to call the police,' he said, jabbing at the carpet with his walking stick.

'Let me speak with him first.'

Charlie opened his mouth to argue but then realised it would be pointless. He turned and headed for the door, cursing under his breath.

He walked down the corridor towards the dining room, his knuckles whitening as he gripped the handle of his walking stick. Billy and Archie were already at the table. Billy was pouring tea and Archie was spreading margarine on what passed for toast.

'Good morning, mate,' said Archie. 'You'll be glad to know that I've popped an extra couple of Tetley's finest in the pot so we've got real tea today.'

Charlie sat down, leant his stick against the wall, folded his arms, and cursed.

'What's wrong, mate?' asked Archie.

'I caught Connolly fiddling with Mrs Chalmers on camera and she won't do a fucking thing about it.'

'That bear thing you bought?' asked Archie, putting down his knife.

'Yeah. The Nanny-cam. Caught the fucker bang to rights fiddling with her but Mrs Woodhouse says she wants to talk to him before calling the cops in.'

'The cops?' repeated Archie. 'I'm not sure that's a great idea, mate.'

'That bastard needs putting away.'

Everton came over with toast for Charlie.

'Hey, Everton, when is Connolly in?' asked Charlie.

'He's on nights for the next week. He asked to be switched.'

Charlie sneered. 'I bet he did.'

'What do you mean?'

Charlie forced a smile. 'Nothing. It's okay. Forget it.'

Everton shrugged his massive shoulders and walked away.

'Do you think he knows what Connolly is doing?' asked Archie, nodding at Everton.

'They're worked off their feet, they don't have time to look around,' said Billy.

'Nah, I think they all know,' said Charlie. 'Mrs Woodhouse definitely knows. She's protecting him.'

Archie spread jam on his toast. 'We need a day at the races,' he said. 'That'll cheer us up.'

CHAPTER 18

'You're a madman,' said Charlie. 'You are the maddest person I know, and I've met a few crazies in my time.'

'I said I wanted a day at the races, and this is the best I could do,' said Archie.

They were standing on the beach. The tide was coming in but it was hundreds of metres away. In the distance the man in the Russian hat had lined up the donkeys and was waiting patiently while a group of teenagers climbed up onto the saddles and prepared to ride. Archie had found the kids in the amusement arcade on the pier and given them a tenner each to go along with his plan. The owner of the donkeys had been reluctant at first but his tune had changed when Archie had slipped him fifty quid.

Archie handed around cigarettes and they stood smoking as the kids got ready, and finally the owner raised his hand. 'They're under starter's orders,' said Archie. 'Place your bets.'

'I'm going for the big one on the end, the brown and white one,' said Charlie.

'Good choice,' said Archie, 'but the jockey looks a bit overweight.'

'I'll have the black one in the middle, the one ridden by the kid with the baseball cap,' said Billy.

'And I'll have the brown one, second from the right,' said Archie. 'I'm impressed with her form.' He blew smoke up at the sky, then raised his left hand and waved at the donkey owner. A second later and the donkeys were trotting across the sand.

The three men cheered on the donkeys and the kids were hollering and kicking their animals to get them to move faster. Archie had promised the winner an extra twenty pounds.

Charlie's choice was in the lead but then the donkey began to tire. A white donkey moved into the lead but then Archie's brown donkey picked up the pace. Archie began cheering at the top of his voice. 'Come in, girl, you can do it!'

Billy was screaming at his donkey and it started to overtake the rest. It made it to second position and then it was neck and neck with Archie's choice. The two donkeys were level for about ten seconds but then the black one edged ahead, urged on by the screaming teenager on its back. 'Go on you beauty!' shouted Billy.

As the pack ran by the three men, the black donkey was still in the lead and Billy had shouted so much that he'd started coughing and spluttering.

Charlie had bent over with laughter and was holding his stick with both hands. 'That was hilarious,' he gasped.

Archie went over to the winner and gave the lad twenty quid. The owner of the donkeys jogged over and started rounding them up.

Billy was still coughing and Archie patted him on the back. 'You okay, mate?' he asked.

'I'm okay,' wheezed Billy. 'Fuck me, that was a riot.'

Charlie straightened up. There were tears running down his cheeks. 'You're crazy,' he said to Archie.

'Just wanted to brighten our day,' said Archie. 'There's too much doom and gloom in that place. Right, come on, the fish and chips are on me.'

They went up the stone steps to the promenade and climbed back on to their scooters. They drove to a fish and chip shop and parked outside. Archie went in and came out with three lots of fish and chips and cans of shandy.

'Shandy?' said Charlie, looking at his can.

'It's the perfect beverage for fish and chips,' said Archie. 'Everyone knows that.'

They drove the scooters back to the promenade and onto the south pier, parking at the end so that they could look out over the sea. 'On a clear day you can see Dublin,' said Archie, breaking off a piece of cod and putting it in his mouth.

'Really?' said Billy.

Archie grinned. 'No mate. Just winding you up.'

'You like a laugh, don't you?' said Charlie.

'Life's too short to take it seriously,' said Archie. 'We've all done our three score and ten. We're all on borrowed time.'

Billy chewed on a chip. 'That's one way of looking at it.'

'He's right,' said Charlie. 'The average age that people die in the UK is just over 81. So yeah, every day is a bonus.'

'I did hear that the average age of a person who died of covid was 82,' said Archie.

'That can't be right,' said Billy. A seagull soared over his head, eyeing his chips.

'No, it's a fact. People who died with the virus were on average a year and a half older than people who died from all the other things that people die of. It targeted old folk, and the fucking government knew it. They knew it and they still sent the virus into the care homes.' Charlie threw a chip into the air and a seagull grabbed it and flew off to the main pier building to eat in peace. 'You know who we should kill? Boris fucking Johnson. Or the fucking idiot who was health minister. Matt what's his fucking name.'

'Matt Hancock,' said Archie.

'Yeah, that's him. I'd love to slice him to pieces.'

'You can't kill anyone in the public eye,' said Billy. 'They never stop looking.'

'That guy got away with killing Jill Dando,' said Charlie. 'It can be done.'

'Jill Dando?' said Billy.

'TV presenter who was shot on her doorstep in 1999,' said Archie. 'They never found her killer.'

'There you go then,' said Charlie. 'She was one of the most famous faces in the country and they never got her killer.'

Archie laughed. 'And on that basis you want to have a crack at Boris Johnson?' He pursed his lips and nodded. 'You know what, we could give it a go. We could ride these scooters down the M6 all the way to Downing Street. What would your weapon of choice be?'

'I'd like to stick something long and sharp up his arse,' said Charlie.

'I've got to be honest, mate, I don't think that's going to happen,' said Archie. He popped another piece of fish into his mouth, chewed and swallowed. 'What was your best?'

'My best?' asked Charlie.

'Your best kill,' said Archie. 'The one you always think about. The one that gets you hard.'

'You are a laugh, Archie. You really are.'

'Come on, we've all got our favourites.'

'What's yours then?' asked Billy.

'Mine?' Archie nodded slowly. 'That would be Lizzie Barnsley. Like the town. She was a secretary. Had a tattoo of a dolphin on one ankle.'

'Why is she your favourite?' asked Charlie.

'The way she begged for her life,' said Archie. 'She'd say anything I told her to say. Anything. And she sounded as if she meant it.'

'In her place?' asked Charlie.

Archie shook his head. 'I had a van. I'd made it look like a van used by a plumbing company in Leeds. It was a Transit, white, with their name and logo on the side and their phone number. Then I had fake number plates made up to match the numbers of the vans the company used. This was more than forty years ago so there wasn't as much CCTV and they didn't have automatic number plate recognition but if they had ever gotten my registration number it wouldn't have got them anywhere.'

He popped a chip into his mouth. 'I'd fitted the van out with four hooks, one in each corner, so that I could tie them up and have them spreadeagled. And I had three single mattresses in the back. No one ever asked but if they had I'd just say I was delivering them for a friend. Then when I was hunting, I'd put two of the mattresses on their sides and that would add soundproofing. I had all the tools I needed. Gags. Chains. Paddles for a bit of slap and tickle. Rohypnol to keep them quiet.'

'The date rape drug?' said Charlie. 'Does it work?'

'Like a dream, mate. I used to use it to catch them, but I'd keep giving it them to keep them quiet.' He grinned. 'I was going through my God phase, you know? I thought I was invincible. She was my seventh. You know what the first couple are like. You're in uncharted waters and learning on the job. Then afterwards you're sure you're going to get caught and every knock on the door is the cops coming to take you away. But by the time you've done five or six, you know the routine. And you get confident. Over confident, maybe. You know that the cops aren't going to catch you unless you do something stupid. You start to feel invincible, right?'

The two men nodded. 'It's like you are God,' said Charlie. 'You get to decide who lives and dies. The power is…'

'Intoxicating,' Archie finished for him. 'Like a drug.'

'Exactly,' said Charlie. 'The best drug in the world. Watching them as they die…' He shuddered with pleasure. 'There's nothing like it.'

'That's how I felt,' said Archie. 'By then I was actively hunting my prey. When I first started I'd take what was available. I'd be out at night and if I saw a girl on her own I'd follow her and attack her if I got the chance. Like a lion, picking off the weaker members of a herd of deer. But once I got more confident I became more selective.' He popped a chip into his mouth and chewed. 'I was a good looking guy back then. I had no problem talking to girls.' He grinned. 'I was a charming fucker, I could talk the birds down off the trees. I used to go to pubs and bars, hunting. Then when I found what I wanted, I'd move in. Bit of chat, buy them a drink or two, feel them out, and then if they fitted the bill I'd slip the roofie into her glass. Not too much, I didn't want her passing out, just enough to make her malleable. Then I'd offer them a lift and once I got them to the van it was all over. Tap them on the head, drag them into the back, tie and gag them and Bob's your uncle. You wouldn't get away with that these days, they'd get the reg off CCTV and that'd be it. But back then you could drive all over the country and provided you didn't run foul of a speed camera, no one would know where you were or where you'd been.'

'What about when you'd finished?' asked Charlie. 'What did you do with the bodies?'

'Back then I used to bury them on Saddleworth Moor, in the Peak District, where Myra Hindley and Ian Brady used to bury their victims. I'd drive along the A635 some days, just to say hello.'

'You never worried about being discovered while you were burying them?' asked Charlie.

'Nah, I had that covered,' said Archie. 'I used to dig the graves days or even weeks before I did the dirty deed. That way if I got caught, I was just digging a hole. That's not a crime, is it? And if I did get spotted, I'd just abandon the hole. I never did though. I used to dig them at night and I'd drive off the road some way so I was never seen. Back in those days the moors were quiet at night, anyway. So I'd dig the grave and then pop back a few days later to check that it hadn't been discovered. If it was good to go, I'd do the dirty deed and take the body there. All I had to do was drop the body in and shovel in the dirt. Took a few minutes and I was out of there.'

Billy nodded. 'Smart.'

Charlie tore off a piece of cod. 'So why was this Lizzie your best kill?' he asked, then put the fish in his mouth.

'Because she lasted so long,' said Archie. 'I parked up in a different part of the moors, about a mile from where I'd dug the grave. I got there about ten thirty at night, and she didn't die until dawn. Three times I thought she was dead but each time she came back. It was like I got four kills for the price of one. She was a fit bitch, was Lizzie. She played squash and there wasn't an ounce of fat on her. But she had perfect breasts. A real handful. I used this ball gag and I had her give one grunt for yes and two grunts for no. We had quite the conversation.' He tossed a chip onto the ground and two seagulls fought over it. The victor flew off and the loser stared reproachfully at

Archie. Archie shrugged at the bird. 'You had your choice, mate,' he said. The bird shrieked at him, flapped its wings and flew off.

'The guy that sold me the roofies had also sold me some Viagra so I was up and at her all night,' he said. 'I kept asking her if she was enjoying it and she had to grunt once or I'd hurt her. I had her grunting all night. I strangled her for the first time after about four hours. I watched the life leak from her eyes and then I released my grip and I thought it was all over but then she started breathing again. A few minutes later and she was awake. So I thought, what the fuck, and I started again. Like I said, it was almost dawn when she finally shuffled off this mortal coil and I had to rush to get her in the hole before the sun came up.' He grinned. 'Happy days.' He chewed on a chip. 'What about you?'

'My favourite?' Charlie chuckled. 'Ah, that would probably be a woman I did in Salford. I fucked up and when I broke in it turned out her husband was home. He was in the merchant navy. Left his cap on the kitchen table. When I'd cased the house he wasn't there, obviously. So I got in and I was halfway up the stairs when I heard him snoring. My heart was thumping, I almost passed out.'

'Fear?'

'No, squire. Excitement. It was a rush. A real rush.'

'You legged it?' asked Billy.

'I almost did,' said Charlie. 'Then I got to the kitchen and saw all these knives in one of those wooden block things. I spent ages looking at those knives, wondering what to do.' He sighed at the memory. 'Eventually I took the biggest.' He held his hands out, about eighteen inches apart. They were shaking. 'It was a big bugger. Big and sharp. Size is important, right? Anyway I went back up the stairs and into the bedroom. I can see it now as if it was yesterday. He was asleep on his back, his mouth open. He was a big man, pot-bellied, clearly liked a drink. She was a slip of a thing, sleeping on her side, her back to the door. So I slipped into the room, went over to the bed, and stuck the knife straight into his heart. He opened his eyes and looked at me but he didn't make a sound, just shuddered and died. He was the first guy I'd killed, it had always been women up until then. First knife, too. I stood looking at the blood spreading around the knife until it dripped down his stomach and started to stain the sheet. I woke her up and showed her what I'd done. The fear in her eyes was something else. It made it so much better. I took the cord from her robe and strangled her with it.'

'You'd didn't fuck her?'

'That wasn't my thing,' said Charlie. 'Sometimes I did but for me it was all about the killing. About watching the life fade from their eyes.'

'I hear you,' said Billy.

'The fact that she died knowing that I'd killed her husband made it that much more exciting,' said Charlie. 'When I'd finished, I put his hands on the knife, making it look like he'd killed himself.'

'The old murder-suicide,' said Archie. 'Nice.'

'It worked,' said Charlie. 'The cops assumed he'd come back from the sea, argued, strangled her and then stabbed himself. It was one of cleanest kills ever, and a double.'

'Did you try it again?' asked Archie. 'A double?'

'Way too risky,' said Charlie. 'That one was a God-send, but trying to do it again would be asking for trouble. I was lucky. But yeah, it's the kill that I'll always remember.'

CHAPTER 19

Archie rolled out of bed and started his exercise regime. Press-ups, sit-ups and some stretching, then he shaved and showered and pulled on clean clothes. He sat down on the bed and picked up the wooden box. He opened it, emptied the contents out on to the bed and then clicked open the secret compartment. His jaw fell when he saw that it was empty. He frowned, unable to believe what he was seeing. The velvet bag was missing. He rubbed the back of his neck. He'd opened the bag the previous morning and the bag had been there then. He had emptied out the rings and they had all been there. 'Bastard,' he muttered. He replaced the compartment, put the items back in the box and placed it on the bedside table. 'Bastard,' he repeated.

He headed to the dining room. Everton was just putting plates down in front of Charlie and Billy. Scrambled eggs and wafer thin slices of cooked ham. Archie sat down and smiled up at Everton. 'Eggs florentine, my man,' he said.

Everyone frowned. 'Say what now?'

'Spinach and poached eggs and Hollandaise sauce served on a fluffy English muffin.'

Everton grinned behind his face screen. 'You kill me, Archie.'

'That could be arranged.'

'Scrambled eggs?'

'Just toast, mate.'

As Everton headed to the kitchen, Archie leaned towards Charlie and Billy. 'That bastard Connolly has stolen my rings.'

'Your trophies?' asked Billy.

'No mate, my cock rings. Yes of course my fucking trophies.'

'You're joking,' said Billy.

'Well if I am you'll have a long wait for the punchline. They were there yesterday afternoon. He must have taken them when he started his shift and we were having our tea.'

Charlie swore. 'I knew that Mrs Woodhouse wouldn't do anything. She doesn't give a fuck.'

'We should tell the police,' said Billy.

Archie looked at him in disgust.

Billy looked down. 'Sorry.'

'We have to do something,' said Charlie.

Archie nodded. 'Tell me about it.'

'We can get them back,' said Charlie.

Archie grimaced. 'How? He'll have taken them home and we don't know where he lives.'

'We can find out.'

'How?'

Charlie grinned. 'I have a cunning plan.'

They finished their breakfasts and headed out to the garden. 'There she is,' said Charlie, nodding towards Mrs Woodhouse who was sitting on a bench talking to one of the residents. 'Looks like she'll be there for a while. Come on.'

They went back inside and along the corridor to Mrs Woodhouse's office. As they reached the door, Sally came around the corner in full PPE, holding a mop and bucket. Billy flashed her a beaming smile. 'Sally, I was looking for you,' he said.

'What do you need, Billy?'

'I'm out of toilet roll. Can you give me a new one?'

Sally frowned. 'You had plenty this morning.'

'I've had the runs. And I'm going to have to go again.' He jiggled from foot to foot.

Sally grinned. 'Okay, come on.'

Charlie waited until Sally and Billy had disappeared around the corner before opening the door to Mrs Woodhouse's office and ushering Archie inside. 'Keep a look out while I open her staff records,' said Charlie, walking over to one of the filing cabinets. He took out his wallet and fished out a small pack of metal picks.

'Are you serious?' said Archie.

'I never go anywhere without them,' said Charlie. 'Now do as I said and keep watch.'

Archie stood by the door while Charlie went to work on the filing cabinet lock. The corridor was clear. Charlie cursed and muttered. 'What's wrong?' whispered Archie.

'My bloody hands,' hissed Charlie. 'The shakes.' He tried again and this time the lock clicked. He pulled open the drawer and rifled through the files, looking for Connolly's. 'Got it,' he said.

Archie looked over his shoulder to see Charlie flicking through the file. When he looked back through the gap in the door, his heart leapt as he saw Mrs Woodhouse walking purposefully towards the office. 'Shit, she's coming,' said Archie.

'I've got the address,' said Charlie. He hurried back to the filing cabinet.

Archie peered through the gap. Mrs Woodhouse was about twenty feet away. 'Shit,' he said. 'Shit, shit, shit.'

He was just about to close the door when he heard Billy down the corridor. 'Mrs Woodhouse!"

She stopped walking and turned to face him, 'Yes, Billy.'

'I've got a complaint.'

'A complaint?'

Billy held up a toilet toll. 'This toilet paper you're giving us. It's terrible.'

Charlie put the file back in the cabinet and closed the door. He crept up behind Archie.

'Terrible in what way?' asked Mrs Woodhouse.

Archie eased open the door. He crept out on tiptoe. Charlie followed him. Mrs Woodhouse was standing with her back to them.

'It's rough,' said Billy. 'Like sandpaper.'

'It's the toilet paper we've always used, Billy.'

Charlie gently closed the door. Then he and Archie tiptoed down the corridor away from Mrs Woodhouse and Billy, holding their breath.

'I need quilted,' said Billy.

'Billy, our budget is stretched as it is, I can't go giving everyone expensive quilted toilet paper.'

She started to turn. Archie and Charlie were still in the corridor and she would see them and know that something was up, so Billy gave a howl and fell to the floor where he began to twitch uncontrollably. As Mrs Woodhouse bent over the twitching Billy, Archie and Charlie hurried around the corner.

CHAPTER 20

Charlie and Archie walked slowly towards Billy's room. The door was ajar and they could hear voices inside. As they got nearer they could see Billy lying on his bed with Mrs Woodhouse and an Indian man with a rumpled grey suit standing over him. They were both wearing covid masks, face shields, and latex gloves. The man also had blue plastic shoe protectors over his footwear

'That's Dr Khan, one of the local GPs,' whispered Charlie.

They moved closer and they could hear the doctor talking to Billy. 'And you've never had anything like this happen before?'

'No, Doc,' said Billy.

'You're taking your blood pressure medication?'

'Every day. First thing.'

'And you're monitoring your glucose levels?'

'Without fail.'

Dr Khan removed his stethoscope and put it in his pocket. 'Have you been under any stress recently? Family problems?'

'I don't have any family left. So no family problems.'

'You're eating regularly?'

'Sure. But you've seen the food here, right? It's not exactly nutritious.'

'Billy!' said Mrs Woodhouse. 'This isn't about our catering arrangements, this is about you collapsing in the corridor.'

'Sorry, Mrs Woodhouse.'

'And no headaches?' asked the doctor. 'No aversion to bright lights?'

'I think I just fainted, Doc.'

113

'It was more than that, Billy,' said Mrs Woodhouse. 'You had a seizure.'

'I'm fine now.'

Mrs Woodhouse looked at Dr Khan. 'As you know, several of our guests do have epilepsy.'

The doctor nodded. 'Indeed. I think we should keep a close eye on Billy and if it happens again, we'll have him in for some tests.'

Billy shook his head vehemently. 'No way are you getting me into hospital.'

'Just for a few tests, so we can see what's going on.'

'Yeah, well I remember covid when everyone who went in, died. And those that didn't, they died when you sent them back.'

'Billy!' said Mrs Woodhouse harshly.

'It's true and you know it's true. Hospitals are where we go to die and I'm not ready to die just yet, thank you very much.' He folded his arms and looked away.

Mrs Woodhouse looked at Dr Khan. 'I'm so sorry about this, Dr Khan. Billy has clearly forgotten his manners.'

'It's quite all right,' said the doctor. 'I can see he's stressed out. We'll just keep an eye on you for the time being, Billy.'

'I'll show you out, Dr Khan,' said Mrs Woodhouse.

As they turned to leave, they saw Archie and Charlie standing in the corridor. 'Yes, gentlemen,' said Mrs Woodhouse. 'Can I help you?'

'We're here to see if Billy's okay,' said Charlie.

'He had a bit of a fall but he's fine,' said Mrs Woodhouse. 'He just needs some rest now.'

'I'm okay, Mrs Woodhouse,' said Billy. 'They'll cheer me up.'

'I'm not sure that's a good idea,' she said.

She looked at the doctor for support but he just shrugged. 'I don't think it'll do any harm,' he said. 'He seems stable now.'

114

Mrs Woodhouse's face tightened but then she forced a smile, nodded, and gestured for the doctor to head down the corridor. She glared at Charlie as she walked by. Charlie smiled amiably and gave her a little wave.

Once they'd gone, Charlie and Archie walked into Billy's room. 'Did you bring grapes, guys?' he asked.

Charlie chuckled as he closed the door. Archie sat down on the end of the bed. 'Did you get Connolly's address?' asked Billy.

'Yeah, we got it,' said Charlie. 'Nice bit of amateur dramatics.'

'I had to do something or she would have turned and seen you.'

'It was perfect, mate,' said Archie.

'So what next?' asked Billy.

'We go to his house and turn it over,' said Charlie. 'It's not far. We can use the scooters.'

'And how do we get in?' asked Billy.

'I was a locksmith, remember?'

'He picked the lock to her filing cabinet, no bother,' said Archie.

Charlie nodded. 'When I was in my prime, there wasn't a lock I couldn't open in two minutes.' He held up his hands. They were trembling. Not much, but there was a definite tremble. 'Now with the Parkinson's, it takes me a bit longer.'

'So back in the day, you never had to break in, right?'

Charlie grinned. 'Yeah, that was my technique. These days they'd call it a signature.'

Archie frowned. 'What, you targeted customers?'

'Hell no, that would have been asking for trouble. That was a rule. I never attacked anyone I'd worked for, or anyone in the area. Cops aren't stupid. They check things like that. I used to find the victim I wanted, then check out their house. Then my thing was to get in while the house was unoccupied.'

'Always houses?'

'Houses are the best bet because if something goes wrong you're on your toes and off down the road. Flats meant you might find yourself stuck on a high floor. But a house, you have a front door and a back door plus windows if you were pushed then you could leg it. Back then, I could run. Boy, could I run.' He sat down on the other side of the bed to Archie. 'For me, it was the anticipation that gave me the kick. Almost as much as the killing. I'd find somewhere to hide so I could listen when they came back. Sometimes I'd listen for hours.' He shuddered with pleasure at the memory. 'My hiding days are over too, I guess. But I can still pick locks, just about.'

Archie nodded thoughtfully. 'Okay, let's do it .'

'When?' asked Billy.

'Let's strike while the iron's hot,' said Archie. 'This evening, as soon as the bastard turns up for work.'

CHAPTER 21

'There he is,' said Billy. They were sitting at their table overlooking the car park, plates of greyish shepherd's pie and pale green peas in front of them. Connolly had parked his car, a ten-year-old VW Polo, and was attaching a security lock to the steering wheel. 'Look at the bastard,' said Billy. 'He's the thief and yet he's the one padlocking his car.'

'Because thieves never trust anyone,' said Archie. 'They assume everyone has the same morals as they do.'

Charlie bolted down the remains of his food, then put down his knife and fork. 'Come on, let's head off while he's putting his gear on.'

They stood up and headed for the door. On the way they walked by Everton, who was serving two old ladies. They had trouble swallowing so their meals always had to be put through a liquidiser and served in bowls. They looked at the green-grey mush with black eyes as they picked up their plastic spoons. 'Not waiting for dessert, lads?' said Everton.

'We're off for a walk,' said Archie. 'Before it gets dark.'

'It's bananas and custard.'

Archie laughed. 'We'll pass,' he said.

They left the dining room and split up to get their coats. Archie was first to reach the scooters and he was sitting on his wearing a dark blue raincoat and a Burberry scarf when the others arrived. Charlie had on a duffel coat and Billy was wearing a denim jacket with Manchester City's logo on the back and a blue and white bobble hat. 'Go the blues,' said Archie.

'Who do you support?' asked Billy as he climbed on his scooter.

'I was always a Blackburn Rovers fan,' said Archie. 'My dad was from Blackburn and he used to take me to matches when I was a kid. But I never went after he died.'

'When was that?'

'Oh, a long time ago,' said Archie. 'I was fifteen. But I still cheer for the Riversiders.'

'Riversiders?' repeated Charlie.

'Yeah, they had a stadium by the river.'

'How did he die?' asked Billy. 'Your dad?'

'I killed him, mate. Smashed his head in with a poker.'

Billy and Charlie looked at him in astonishment. Archie held their look for several seconds before his face cracked into a smile. 'If you could fucking see yourselves,' he said. 'Seriously? You think I'd beat my old man to death with a poker? For fuck's sake.'

Charlie's eyes narrowed. 'So did you? Or didn't you?'

'Of course I didn't. It was a joke. He had a heart attack.' He sighed and shook his head. 'You soft bastards.'

'You looked like you meant it,' said Billy.

'I was pulling your chain,' said Archie.

'Come on, stop pissing around. We've got work to do.' He headed out of the home and Billy and Charlie followed him. They drove into the town, then turned left on the fourth road running parallel to the beach road. The houses were shabby and uncared for and most of the cars parked at the roadside were rusting and scratched. Mothers with toddlers and babies, wrapped up against the evening cold, headed home, more often than not with a cigarette dangling from their chapped lips.

The pavements were narrow so they kept their speed to walking pace. They crossed over the road and then Charlie took them up a side street of terraced houses, several of which had English flags displayed in their windows. The graffiti on some of the walls was mainly initials and signatures. This wasn't Banksy territory, it was a place where working class kids with no futures tried to leave their mark.

There was a Chinese restaurant on one corner but as they got closer they realised it had been boarded up. They went past it in single file. Two teenagers in hoodies were sharing a roll-up in an alleyway and they turned to stare at the scooters. 'Got any spare...' one began but they had already gone by.

A police car was parked ahead of them and Charlie slowed, but before they drew level with it the flashing light came on and the siren burst into life and it drove off with a squeal of tyres.

He took a left and then stopped and waited for the other two to catch up. 'That's the house, over there,' he said, pointing at a rundown semi-detached house with a paved-over front garden that was now used as parking spaces. Three wheelie bins were lined up in front of the ground floor window. 'He's in Flat A which is probably the ground floor. I'll wander over and see how I get on with the lock. We can't all be there, it'll attract too much attention. You guys keep an eye out. Assuming I get the door open, come on over.'

He drove along to the house and onto the parking area, then walked over to the front door. He took his picks from his pocket and began working on the lock. Even from where they were they could see that his hands were shaking.

'So he's got Parkinson's?' said Archie.

'Yeah, he's had it for a while,' said Billy. 'It got a lot worse after he had covid.'

'Do they give him tablets?'

'Yeah, but he doesn't like taking them. Says they play havoc with his memory.'

As they watched, Charlie dropped one of his picks. He bent down slowly to retrieve it. He seemed to lose his balance and had to put a hand against the door to steady himself.

'Shall we go over?' asked Billy.

'He'll be okay,' said Archie. 'He's right, we'll stick out like a sore thumb if we all hang around outside.'

Charlie went back to working on the lock. After just over a minute, he pushed the door open and turned to wave them over.

Archie and Billy drove their scooters over to the house and parked. Charlie ushered them inside and closed the door behind them. There had once been carpet on the flight of stairs to their left but it had been removed. The wallpaper was wood chip painted a pale green, scuffed and ripped and with patches of mould close to the ceiling. Archie wrinkled his nose at the smell of damp.

There was a single door to their right with an A nailed to it and there was only one lock, a Yale. 'Easy peasy,' said Charlie. 'I used to open these with a credit card.' He inserted two picks but as he twisted them one slipped from his fingers and fell to the floor. Charlie cursed.

'I'll get it,' said Archie. He bent down, retrieved the pick and handed it to Charlie.

'Thanks, squire,' said Charlie. He turned back to the lock and within seconds it clicked and he pushed the door open. They slipped inside and Charlie closed the door.

Archie wrinkled his nose again. If anything, the smell was worse in the flat than in the hallway. It was a mess, Connolly clearly didn't bother clearing up after himself. There were dirty clothes thrown everywhere and discarded fast food containers on a small table by the window. The sink was piled high with dirty dishes in the small kitchen. There was no oven, just a microwave and a double hotplate.

A plastic sofa faced a big screen television that was connected to a PlayStation games console on a pine coffee table that was scarred with circular water stains. Posters of topless women dotted the walls and the only reading matter seemed to be graphic novels and comics.

'He's a fucking animal,' said Charlie.

'I think we already knew that,' said Billy.

A plastic door led to a shower room. Archie pushed it open and he almost gagged at the stench of urine and mould.

A second door, this one plywood, led to a small room with a single bed with a grubby duvet and a pillow streaked with grease. The curtains were drawn. Black with white Satanic symbols on them. Charlie laughed out loud. 'Are you kidding me? Black magic curtains?'

'I think they're from some video game,' said Billy.

Archie and Charlie looked at him in surprise. Billy held up his hands. 'I used to play video games, it's not a crime.'

Archie looked around the room. 'So where do you think he'd hide his prizes?'

There was a wardrobe with a mirrored door and a dressing table on which there was a selection of antiperspirants.

'Nowhere too clever because he's not too bright,' said Charlie.

Archie pointed at a suitcase on top of the wardrobe. 'Five'll get you ten that he thinks a locked suitcase will do the job.'

He reached for the suitcase but it was heavy and Billy had to help him get it down onto the bed. It was soft-sided and there was a padlock holding the zip shut. It took Charlie a few seconds to pop the lock.

Archie unzipped the suitcase and lifted the lid to reveal items of women's clothing including a scarf and underwear.

'What a sick fuck,' said Billy.

Archie moved a silk blouse to reveal a metal box. Archie lifted the lid and shook his head. 'Bastard,' he whispered.

Inside the box were watches and jewellery. And the red velvet bag that contained Archie's rings. As Archie picked up the bag, Billy reached into the box and grabbed an old pocket watch. 'This is mine,' he said. 'This is fucking mine. It used to belong to my dad. It went missing while I was in the hospital with covid. They all said I was lying, that I never had a watch. He fucking nicked it. I always knew it.' He put the watch in his pocket.

Charlie picked up a row of medals. 'Fuck me, these must be Melvyn's medals. Looks like he really was a hero.'

Archie opened the red velvet bag and poured the rings into his hand.

'Are they all there?' asked Billy.

Archie nodded.

'Do you think he realises what they are?' asked Charlie.

'He's too stupid,' said Archie. 'I was just lucky he hadn't sold them.'

'He probably knows that if he tries to sell them in Blackpool he'll get caught,' said Charlie.

Archie slipped the rings back into the bag.

'Guys, we need to think about this,' said Charlie.

Billy frowned. 'What do you mean?'

'If you take your stuff back, he'll know we've been here.'

'So?' said Billy. 'Who cares what he knows or doesn't know?'

'No, Charlie's right,' said Archie. 'It'll tip Connolly off. He'll know someone is on to him. He'll either run or dump the stuff.'

'So we go straight to the cops,' said Billy. 'He's a thief and an abuser. The cops will throw away the key.'

'We can't tell the cops,' said Charlie, putting the medals back in the box. 'How do we explain how we got in? And more importantly, how do we explain Archie's trophies? The cops will want to know where the rings came from.'

They all looked at the red velvet bag in Archie's hand. 'He's got a point,' said Billy.

'Like I said, we need to talk about this,' said Charlie. 'We can't let Connolly know we've been here and we can't go to the cops. And we have to keep Connolly in the dark until we decide what we're going to do with him.'

'Okay,' said Archie. 'That makes sense.'

'And that means we can't take anything from his stash. The watch and the rings have to stay here.'

Billy took the watch from his pocket. 'I'm not happy about this,' said Billy. 'It means a lot to me, this watch.'

'I know. But you know this makes sense.'

Billy reluctantly put the watch back in the box. Archie put the red velvet bag next to the watch, then took out his phone and started taking photographs of the contents.

'What are you doing, squire?'

'Evidence,' said Archie. 'Just in case anything goes missing.'

'Good idea,' said Charlie.

Archie took a few more photographs and then put his phone away. Then he picked up the velvet bag and undid the gold cord.

'You need to leave the bag in the box, Archie,' said Charlie.

'I will, but I'm taking one with me.' He fished out one of the rings and held it up. It was the only one without a card attached to it. 'This one is special, that bastard's not having it. Not even for one extra day.'

'Ah, the first one, yeah? The first is always special.'

Archie put the ring in his wallet, then dropped the red bag into the metal box. 'There you go,' he said.

Charlie closed the box, zipped up the suitcase and affixed the padlock. Then he and Archie lifted the suitcase back onto the wardrobe.

'Now what?' said Billy.

'Let's go somewhere quiet for a chat,' said Archie. 'We need to get our ducks in a row.'

CHAPTER 22

They drove their scooters back to the promenade. Archie led the way and he stopped outside a crazy golf course. Charlie and Billy parked either side of him. 'Are you serious?' asked Charlie.

'My treat,' said Archie. 'We can talk as we play.'

He climbed off his scooter and went over to a shed where a woman in a bright red Puffa jacket and a multicoloured Tibetan wool hat took his money and gave him three old putters, three golf balls and cardboard score sheets and pencils.

Charlie laughed as Archie gave him a club and a ball. 'You're a nutter,' he said.

The first hole had to be played through a six-foot tall windmill, whose sails brushed the ground and blocked the hole. Charlie played first. His timing was spot on and the ball shot through the tunnel in the windmill, came out of the other side, bounced off a side wall and plopped into the hole. 'We should play for money,' he said.

Billy was up next but his timing was off and it took him three shots to get through the windmill and another two to get the ball in the hole. Archie managed it in two shots. They all scribbled their scores on their cards and walked over to the second hole. This involved sending the ball over a hump-backed bridge with a large hole in it. If the ball went down the hole it ended up back at the start.

'So what do you think?' asked Charlie.

'I'd hit it hard and to the left,' said Archie.

'About Connolly, I mean,' said Charlie. 'He's the perfect candidate. We get to scratch our itch and we rid the world of a scumbag.'

'So now we're vigilantes?'

'He stole your trophies.'

'So we take them back. And Billy's watch. And Melvyn's medal. And everything else he stole.'

Charlie leaned on his club. 'And then what?'

'We tell the cops,' said Archie. 'Send an anonymous letter or make a call to Crimestoppers.'

Charlie shook his head. 'I already gave the CCTV to Mrs Woodhouse and she did nothing about it.'

'So we send the CCTV to the cops and let them handle it. What do you think, Billy?'

'I want to kill the bastard,' said Billy. 'And I want to make him suffer.'

'You're missing the point, Archie,' said Charlie. He hit the ball and it went straight to the hole at the top of the bridge, dropped down, and a few seconds later reappeared at his feet.

'And you're missing the hole.'

'The point is, I want to kill someone, Archie. It's been almost fifteen years.'

'And none of us are getting any younger,' said Billy.

'Well that much at least is true,' said Archie. 'But the first rule of serial killing, remember? You never shit on your own doorstep.'

Charlie took his second shot and this time it went over the bridge. It rolled by the hole and stopped about three feet away. 'That's not written in stone.' He took up position over the ball, turned his head from side to side, then took his shot, He cursed as he missed it by a good six inches. 'This club's shit,' he said.

'You can use mine, mate,' said Archie.

'Yours is shit, too.' Charlie tried again and this time the ball dropped into the hole.

'Says it's a par two,' said Archie, looking at the score card.

'Let's see you do it in two, then,' said Charlie.

Archie put his ball down, eyed up the hole in the bridge and the hole he was aiming for, then took his shot. It skirted the hole in the bridge, rolled past the target hole, then hit the wall and bounced back and dropped in. 'That'd be a hole in one, I think,' he said.

'Bastard,' said Charlie.

'You say shitting on your own doorstep isn't written in stone,' said Archie quietly. 'Have you ever killed someone you knew?'

'No. But that's not the point.'

'It's exactly the point. If you kill someone you know there's a connection and if there's a connection, Plod will find it.'

Billy hit his ball. It missed the hole in the bridge and came to a halt a couple of feet from the target hole. 'If you're careful, you can get away with it,' he said.

'Crap,' said Archie. 'Connolly is out of bounds. We can turn him into the cops, but if we kill him, we'll get caught. I don't want to spend what few years I've got left behind bars. Not for a shit like Connolly, anyway.'

Billy walked over to his ball and tapped it into the hole. 'It's doable. You can get away with killing someone you know. I did it once.'

Charlie narrowed his eyes. 'You never said.'

'You never asked.'

'Come on then,' said Charlie. 'Spill the beans.'

Billy upended his club and leaned on it as if it was a walking stick. 'Her name was Sarah. She was my fifteenth so I was pretty well organised by then. She ran a bookshop in Norwich. She was little with perfect tits and blonde hair down to her waist. My type. Exactly my type. But, like you said, you don't kill someone you know. I fantasied about it for years, you know? Like you do.'

Archie and Charlie nodded.

'And then one time, I was driving towards Norwich. I was calling on three bookshops there and she was on my list. She'd stopped in a lay-by and was obviously having car trouble. So I made an on the spot decision. Spur of the moment.'

Charlie shook his head. 'An impulse buy? Never a good idea.'

126

'I didn't have time to think,' said Billy. 'If I had thought it through then I'd probably not have done it. Back then I was using a stun gun and I had it in the glove box. So I get the stun gun and I pull up. She'd run out of petrol so I said I'd take her to a garage. She got in. I didn't have long to make up my mind but make up my mind I did.'

'You zapped her?' said Charlie.

Billy nodded. 'Yeah. Gave her the full Monty, right in the neck. She went out like a light. Took her to a wooded area to the north of the city. Raped her and killed her. A perfect kill. Then I buried the body. And that's the key.'

Archie frowned. 'The key?'

'To not getting caught. I buried the body so carefully that no one could ever find it. So with no body, there's always the possibility that she ran off. New boyfriend, new life. And without a body, there's no evidence. Not that I left any DNA behind. I never did.'

'But you took a trophy?' said Archie.

'Always,' said Billy. 'But you see my point? If the cops have a body then they know what happened and they pull out all the stops. But without a body, there's always doubt. There's always the possibility that the person just went away.'

'And they never looked at you?' asked Archie. 'For her disappearance?'

'No one saw me pick her up. No one saw me kill her. No one saw me bury the body. I turned up at her shop and her staff said she hadn't been in. I took an order from her assistant and that was that. Cops never even spoke to me. But you see what I'm getting at, right?'

'You're saying we can kill Connolly if we get rid of the body?' said Charlie.

'Exactly. If he just goes missing, the cops won't be bothered. In fact they might think he's done a runner because of the CCTV footage you got.'

Charlie looked over at Archie. 'What do you think?'

Archie shrugged. 'I think you never shit on your own doorstep, that's what I think.'

127

'But if we get rid of the body so that no one finds it?'

Archie shrugged again, then he sighed. 'Okay. Yeah. Maybe.'

CHAPTER 23

The next morning, after breakfast, they drove their scooters to a large do-it-yourself store some two miles from the home. They were wearing their coats and scarves and Billy had his Manchester City bobble hat on. They parked on the pavement and walked inside. 'Can I help you guys?' asked a young sales assistant in a brown coat who was barely out of his teens.

'We're good,' said Archie. 'Just browsing.'

They walked over to a display of power tools. Charlie picked up a sturdy circular saw. 'Made in Germany,' he said. 'Vorsprung durch Technik.'

'What does that mean?' asked Billy.

'It's the Audi slogan,' said Charlie. 'Getting ahead through technology.'

'Have either of you done this before?' asked Archie.

'Done what?' asked Charlie.

Archie pointed at the saw. 'You know what.'

'I haven't, but how hard can it be?'

'I was a butcher, remember? I can tell you, it's not easy. And it's messy.'

Charlie grinned. He mimed using the saw on Archie. 'You take off the head, the arms and the legs, bish, bash, bosh. And you do it in the bath.'

'And then what?' asked Archie.

'Then you dispose of it. Dump it somewhere secluded.'

'Sure. And then someone finds it and the cops go mental.'

'So we bury the bits. Bury them deep.'

Archie flashed him a thin smile. 'Where? On the beach?

Charlie sighed in frustration. 'We find a forest or something. The Lake District. Or your old stamping ground. The moors.'

'And what, we get an Uber? Hi mate, let me just put these black bags in the boot and don't worry about the smell.'

Charlie put the circular saw down and picked up a chain saw.' 'I don't understand why you're being so negative.'

'I'm being practical, mate,' said Archie.

'Maybe you should be thinking creatively,' said Charlie. 'Put it through a mincer. Like you mince meat.'

Archie shook his head. 'You can't mince a skull. Or a hip.'

'What about acid?' said Billy. 'We could dissolve the bits in acid.'

Charlie put down the chain saw and they went over to a display of drain cleaners and bleach. Billy pricked up a five litre bottle of bleach. 'Do you think this'll dissolve flesh?'

Archie nodded at a female assistant who was stocking shelves in the next aisle. 'You could ask her.'

Billy turned towards her and Archie pulled him back, chuckling. 'I was joking, mate.'

'I knew that,' said Billy, putting the bottle back on the shelf.

'Anyway, bleach won't dissolve flesh or bone,' said Archie. 'You need a really strong acid for that and something to put it in. We can hardly use one of the baths in the home, can we? It takes time.'

Charlie nodded. 'Yeah, it'll take forever. There's the skull, the bones. The teeth.'

'So we cut it into small pieces and then use the acid,' said Billy.

'And then what?' said Archie. 'Pour it down the toilet?'

Charlie nodded. 'That would work.'

'Until there's a blockage somewhere and the Dyno-Rod guy finds a pile of teeth,' said Archie. 'This is crazy.'

Charlie threw up his hands in frustration. 'Then you come up with something.'

'That's what I'm trying to tell you, it's not like it used to be. Back in the day I'd drive up to the moors and drop the body in a hole. But back then there was no CCTV, no number plate recognition. And let's face it, even if it was an option the only transport we've got are the scooters and I don't rate our chances of taking Connolly's body anywhere on a scooter.'

'So we cut the body up,' said Billy.

'And where do we do that?'

'His place. We kill him in his flat and chop him up in the bathroom. Then we dispose of the pieces. It doesn't have to be in the moors, not if we've got small bits.'

'That could work, Archie,' said Charlie. 'Cut him into small pieces with a saw, wrap them up and drop them in skips or bins.'

Archie looked at the two men, nodding slowly. 'Maybe we're overthinking it,' he said. 'Come on, let's get some fresh air.'

They went back to the scooters and drove to the North Pier. It was the oldest of the town's three piers, with a wide deck, a theatre and a carousel. Archie bought them all cockles and whelks and then they drove to the shadow of the carousel and parked looking out over the sea.

'What if we leave the body in plain view?' asked Archie.

Billy squinted at him. 'What do you mean?'

'I mean we don't try to hide it. But we make it look like something else happened.'

'Like an accident? Yeah, that would work.'

'He lives in a ground floor flat,' said Charlie. 'It's not like he can fall down stairs or out of a window, is it?'

'No,' said Archie. 'But we could make it look like he killed himself.'

'Hang him, you mean?' said Billy. 'Or tablets? Poison? Or slash his wrists.'

'The simpler the better,' said Archie. 'We could make it look like that auto-asphyxiation thing. Put a plastic bag over his head.'

Charlie nodded. 'I like the sound of that.'

'Me too,' said Billy.

Archie grinned. 'Me three.'

CHAPTER 24

They arrived back at the home and parked their scooters by the back door. 'I want to show you something,' said Billy.

Archie and Charlie followed him past Mrs Woodhouse's office and around the corner to a door with a sign that read STORAGE ROOM. Billy opened it. The room was about ten feet square and lined with metal shelving filled with supplies the home needed, including toilet rolls, disinfectant, detergent and washing up liquid. Archie stepped inside and waved for them to join him.

He pointed at a line of boxes. 'Masks,' he said. 'Facemasks, The clear plastic ones.' He opened a box and took one out.

'We know what masks are, Billy,' said Charlie.

Billy pointed at another box. 'Latex gloves.' He waved at a box on the floor. 'Plastic overalls, just like the ones that the CSIs wear.'

'SOCO,' said Archie. 'They call them SOCO in the UK. Scene Of Crime Officers. Only Yanks call them Crime Scene Investigators.'

Billy rolled his eyes. 'CSI, SOCO, that's not the point. The point is that we can use this gear when we do Connolly. That way there'll be no forensics. The idea is to make it look like he topped himself, right? So that means we mustn't leave any DNA or fingerprints or hair. So we use this gear when we do the dirty deed. Right?'

'It makes sense,' said Charlie. 'There doesn't seem to be any stock control here, we can take what we need.'

'I'm convinced,' said Archie. He looked at his watch. 'Time for lunch.'

They went through to the dining room. Raja and Sally were serving, and it was Raja who brought over their food. Macaroni cheese from a packet and frankfurter sausages.

Archie smiled up at him. 'Raja, can I ask you a question?'

Raja sighed. 'Don't start on about the food, Archie. I'm not in the mood today.'

'It's not that, mate.' He leaned closer to him. 'You know what Connolly is up to, right?'

'What are you talking about?'

'He's abusing the vulnerable women in here. You've seen how he messes them around.'

Raja frowned. 'Abuse is a bit strong, Archie.'

'What would you call it?' asked Archie.

'This isn't the easiest of jobs,' said Raja. 'No offence intended.'

Archie grinned. 'I know we have a habit of breaking your balls, Raja, but that comes from affection. We like you.'

'You're one of the good guys, Raja,' said Billy. 'We all say that.'

'Well that's nice of you, if I need a reference I'll know where to come.'

'You know he's a thief?' said Archie.

'Who? Jackie? What's he been stealing? Because nobody here has two pennies to rub together.'

'Jewellery. Watches. Anything of value.'

'Archie, with the best will in the world, nobody here has anything of value.'

'He stole my watch,' said Billy. 'When I was in hospital with the covid.'

'Why didn't you report it?'

'I didn't know. I was confused. The virus fucked me up. It fucked everybody up.'

'How do you know it was Jackie who stole your watch?' asked Raja.

Billy opened his mouth to answer but Charlie silenced him with a warning look and a shake of the head. 'I just know,' mumbled Billy.

'It's generally known,' said Archie.

'By who?'

Charlie and Archie exchanged a look. There was no way they could tell Raja what they had seen in Connolly's bedroom. 'What about the abuse?' asked Archie. 'You must have seen what he does to Mrs Chalmers. He teases her when he's feeding her, he slops food on her face.'

'Mrs Chalmers has dementia, feeding her is problematical at the best of times.'

'It's more than that, Raja, and you know it,' said Archie. 'He's fucking with her. He's always fucking with her.'

Raja looked around to check that no one else was within earshot. 'If he was, what am I supposed to do about it?'

'You could report him.'

'So it would be my word against his,' said Raja. 'And between you and me, he's got a temper.'

'You're afraid of him?' asked Archie.

'Not at the moment, no. But that could change if he heard that I'd complained about him. Like I said, he's got a temper. And Mrs Woodhouse is a fan.'

'Yeah, we know that,' said Charlie. 'We got him on tape abusing Mrs Chalmers in her room and she didn't do a thing about it.'

Raja's jaw dropped. 'You did what?'

'We put a Nanny-cam in her room.'

'When he says "we" he means he did,' said Billy.

'He was caught on tape but she couldn't care less,' said Charlie.

'Just let it drop, guys,' said Raja. 'He can make life miserable for all of us. You don't want him on your case, and I need this job.'

'How long have you been here, Raja?' asked Archie.

'I signed up in the middle of the second wave of the virus,' he said. 'I used to run an Indian in the Curry Mile, but it went out of business.'

The Curry Mile was a stretch of Wilmslow Road running through the Rusholme area of South Manchester with more than seventy restaurants and takeaways crammed into half a mile.

'We made it through the first wave just about, but the second wave did the real damage, especially when they locked down all the students. The owner went back to Bangladesh and I came here.' He leaned closer to their table. 'I'm serious, guys. I need this job. I was lucky to get it. My family depends on me, you know what the economy's like at the moment. So whatever you're planning to do about Mr Connolly, please leave me out of it.'

'We hear you, Raja,' said Archie.

'Thanks, guys,' said Raja. He walked away.

Archie toyed with his food. 'It's a pity he wasn't a chef in the Curry Mile,' he said.

'I love a good curry, me,' said Billy.

'What's the plan, guys?' asked Charlie.

'We eat this and maybe have a few games of dominoes?' said Archie.

Charlie lowered his voice. 'You know what I mean. Connolly. Are you up for it. We get to scratch our itch and do the home a favour at the same time.'

Archie took a deep breath and then sighed. 'How about we sleep on it?'

'Sleep on it?' repeated Charlie.

'Let's just take a breath, yeah? Think about it overnight and see how we feel in the morning.'

Charlie nodded slowly. 'Okay. But I'm not going to change my mind.'

CHAPTER 25

Archie buttoned up his pyjama jacket and climbed into bed. His wallet was on his bedside table and he leaned over and opened it and took out the wedding ring. It was the only one without a label attached to it, but he didn't need anything to remind him of who it had belonged to. He would have liked to have worn it but it was too small to fit on any of his fingers.

He lay back and held the ring tightly. Sometimes, if he was lucky, he would dream about her, but, even if he didn't, having the ring in his grasp seemed to intensify the memories. He closed his eyes and was soon snoring softly.

He woke up at seven-thirty on the dot and lay on his back staring up at the ceiling for several minutes. He hadn't dreamed about her. He hadn't dreamed about anything. He realised that he wasn't holding the ring and his heart pounded. He sat up but found it immediately, on the duvet by his knees. He picked it up and kissed it, then put it back in his wallet.

He showered, shaved and dressed and went along to the dining room, where Billy and Charlie were already sitting at their table. As Archie joined them, Everton came over with two plates with scrambled eggs and square slices of cooked ham. Archie grimaced at the lacklustre food. 'Just toast for me, Everton. The eggs look….' He shrugged and didn't bother finishing the sentence.

Everton grinned. 'I've got a surprise for you.'

'Mate, a surprise is the last thing I need right now, he said. 'Toast is fine, just try to make sure it is actually toasted and not just warmed.'

Everton chuckled as he walked away.

Charlie poured supermarket ketchup onto his eggs. 'I spoke to Mrs Woodhouse first thing. She says not to worry and that she's handling it.'

'Do you believe her?' asked Archie.

Charlie snorted. 'Of course not.'

'If you did, I've got a bridge I can sell you,' said Billy. He shovelled a forkful of eggs into his mouth.

Charlie screwed the cap back on the sauce bottle. 'The bitch is lying through her teeth. I asked her for the bear and she said she'd sent it to her boss, and I don't believe that either. She's done away with the evidence, that's what she's done.' He banged the sauce bottle down on the table. 'Bitch!'

'How about we do her, too?' said Billy. 'Buy one, get one free.'

Charlie nodded enthusiastically. 'We could do. Yeah, why not?'

'Guys, get a grip will you?' said Archie. 'This isn't a bloody game.'

Everton returned with two triangles of toast in a stainless steel rack and a plate which he put down in front of Archie with a flourish. Archie's eyes widened when he saw what it was. Two perfectly-poached eggs on a bed of spinach on top of toasted muffins. 'Eggs florentine! You are fucking kidding me!'

Everton grinned behind his face shield. 'Paul in the kitchen used to work at a big hotel in Leeds. Had a word and he said he'd see what he could do.' He lowered his head. 'But don't let Mrs Woodhouse know. Mum's the word.'

'I won't be telling anyone, Everton,' said Archie. 'And my compliments to the chef.'

Archie picked up his knife and fork and beamed at Charlie and Billy. 'How about this, then?'

He cut through one of the eggs and the yolk flowed down over the muffin. 'Would you look at that,' he said. 'That right there is perfection on a plate.'

'So what are your plans today, after you've finished your feast?' asked Charlie.

'Thought I might go for a drive in my limo. Take in the sights.' He popped egg, spinach and muffin into his mouth and sighed contentedly.

Charlie grinned. 'Always the fucking joker,' he said. He leaned across the table. 'We need to get planning.' He looked left and right and lowered his voice. 'The Connolly thing.'

Archie nodded. 'Sure.'

'We need a plan,' said Charlie. 'We need equipment. We need alibis.'

Archie shrugged. 'The equipment is in the supply room. I'm sure you'll work the rest of it out.'

'We're a team,' said Charlie. 'We're all in this together.'

'Absolutely,' said Archie. 'Birds of a feather.' He cut into the second egg and smiled as the yolk oozed over the spinach. 'Perfect,' he said.

'So we need to start thinking as a team,' said Charlie. 'I was thinking about porn.'

Archie grinned. 'Were you now?'

Charlie threw him a withering look. 'I mean, we could set it up so that it looks as if Connolly was watching porn when he self-asphyxiates. Make it a sexual thing.'

'Ah,' said Archie. 'Okay.'

'First I thought we could make it a suicide thing but that wouldn't fly. But porn... the cops would buy that. He was tossing himself off with a bag over his head - it happens.'

'Not in my world it doesn't,' said Archie with a sly grin.

'Or mine,' said Billy.

Billy and Archie chuckled. Charlie held up a hand to silence them. 'I did try it once.'

Billy frowned. 'You what?'

'You tried to suffocate yourself?' said Archie.

'Don't be stupid,' said Charlie. 'Why would I do that? No, I meant I did it to one of my victims.' He leaned forward and lowered his voice. 'I put a bag over her head before I started raping her. The bitch died before I came, but it was still one hell of a rush.'

139

Billy nodded enthusiastically. 'You the man.'

Charlie grinned. 'I was. I was most definitely the man.'

'So are you thinking magazines or what?' asked Archie.

'Magazines won't work because they're traceable and most shops have got CCTV these days. But we could get it on his computer.'

'Was there a computer in his flat?' said Archie. 'I only saw the PlayStation console.'

'Good point,' said Charlie. 'Can you get porn on a PlayStation?'

'I'm not sure, but we could definitely get it on his phone,' said Billy.

'But his phone will be password protected,' said Archie.

Billy shook his head. 'Nah, he's got one of those new Apple phones that does facial recognition. I've seen him use it.'

'So we can unlock the phone after he's dead?' asked Charlie.

'I don't see why not,' said Billy. 'And we can call up a porn site and leave that running. The cops will see the porn and the bag over his head and put two and two together.'

'Have you guys given any thought as to how we do it, though?' asked Archie. 'He's not going to put his head in a plastic bag just because we tell him, is he? And we're going to have to do it at his flat, right? How are we going to do that? Just knock on his door and ask him if we can come in?'

'Obviously not,' said Charlie.

'So what's the plan?' asked Archie.

'I was thinking we should drug him. Once he's out we can put the bag over this head, use duct tape to seal it around his neck and bob's your uncle.'

'The duct tape would be a red flag to the cops,' said Archie.

'What do you mean?'

'Would a guy practising auto-asphyxiation use duct tape? How's he going to undo it when he's finished?'

'Good point,' said Charlie. 'So rope, then?'

'Rope would work,' said Archie. 'But we're putting the cart before the horse. How are we going to drug him? We can't drug him here because he'll never get home.'

'Could we do it here?' asked Billy. 'The whole thing?'

'Too many people,' said Charlie. 'And besides, he's not going to try auto-asphyxiation here, is he? It's the sort of thing you do at home.' He saw the smirk flash across Archie's face. 'And no, that isn't the voice of experience talking.'

'So we have to drug him at home.'

'Right, which brings me back to my first point. How do we get in?'

'I can get us in, same as I did last time.'

'And then what? We all hide in the bathroom?'

'We could get into his flat and put it in whatever he drinks,' said Charlie.

'Put what in?' asked Archie.

'That's the easy bit,' said Charlie. 'Half the people in here are dosed up to the eyeballs on tranquillisers. All we have to do is snaffle a few pills.' He spread margarine on a slice of toast. 'But yeah, we need to think about how we get the drugs into his system.'

'What does he drink?' asked Archie.

'We should have checked his fridge while we were in his flat,' said Billy.

'He drinks coffee,' said Charlie. 'So we could drug his milk.'

'What milk?' asked Archie.

'Presumably he has milk in the fridge,' said Charlie.

'What if he doesn't?' asked Archie.,

'Well we get in and have a look,' said Charlie. 'If there's milk, we can put it in his milk. Or in his kettle.'

'Can you boil sedatives or does the heat destroy them?' asked Archie.

Charlie sighed in annoyance. 'You seem to be throwing up a lot of roadblocks, squire.'

'Perfect planning prevents piss-poor performance, remember? Best we iron out the wrinkles now rather than trying to think on our feet later.'

'You just seem very negative, that's all.'

Archie shook his head. 'No, mate. Just careful. There's no point in doing this if we end up getting caught. We've all had perfect records so far, we don't want to fuck it up with our last hurrah.'

'Who says this is the last one,' said Billy. 'This is a trial run, right? If we can do Connolly, we can do others.'

'One step at a time,' said Archie. He finished his breakfast and put down his knife and fork. 'You know my thoughts on shitting on our own doorstep, But Connolly is a prick and we'll be doing everyone a favour by offing him so I'm up for it, providing we can thrash out the details. What I don't want is for it all to go tits up and we end up behind bars. Because if that happens and they start digging - literally or figuratively - then we open up a whole can of worms. But I'm not being negative. I want to scratch my itch every bit as much as you guys do.'

'Good to know,' said Charlie. 'But you don't seem happy with the plan.'

'Because it's not really a plan, is it? Pop tranquillisers in his kettle in the hope that he drugs himself. How would we know if he's drunk it or if it's worked? Knock on his door? And if he answers, what then?' He shook his head. 'We're leaving too much to chance.'

'So what's your idea?' asked Billy.

Archie took two teabags from his pocket and popped them into the stainless steel teapot.

'You know, I prefer Yorkshire Tea,' said Charlie.

'Nah, but it has to be Tetleys,' said Archie. 'More flavour.'

'No, no, no,' said Billy. 'PG Tips is the best. There's no comparison. And they have the triangular bags which means you get more flavour out of them.'

142

'That's just a marketing gimmick,' said Charlie.

Archie grinned. 'Fuck me, we can't even agree over what teabags to use and here we are trying to plan a murder.'

'Shhh!' said Charlie, looking around. 'Don't say that.'

'Relax, Charlie, no one's listening,' said Archie. He used a teaspoon to prod the teabags and stir the tea in the pot. 'Look, I think you're right about the auto-asphyxiation thing. That's probably the way to go. My first thought was that we dress up in the PPE gear, wait for him to get back and then beat him over the head with the proverbial blunt instrument, then make it look as if he'd slipped in the shower and banged his head.'

'That could work,' said Billy.

Archie shook his head. 'If we could be sure of sneaking up on him, maybe,' he said. 'But the only place to hide is in the bathroom. He's a big fellah so it would probably take all three of us, which means we'd all be in the bathroom. Suppose he heads straight there for a pee? Then we're all trapped there and we can only go through the door one at a time.'

'So we go the tranquilliser route, like I said.'

'Yeah, I hear you. And in a perfect world it'd work. He comes home, makes himself a cup of coffee, drugs himself and passes out.' He poured tea into his cup and added a splash of milk. 'Except how do we know he's passed out? We could call him but then there'll be a record of the call. And what if we have to call several times? Or we could knock on the door but what if he answers? Then we're blown. There are too many variables.' Charlie opened his mouth to speak but Archie silenced him with a wave of his hand. 'I know, I know, I'm being negative. But how about this? One of us gets into the flat and hides in the bathroom, full PPE so there's no forensics, and he'd got a hypodermic full of the tranquilliser. There's loads of hypodermics here, right?'

The two men nodded.

'So, one of us is inside. The other two keep watch outside. As soon as he lets himself into the flat, one of the other two rings the bell. There's no intercom so he has to open the door to his flat and then go into the hallway and open the front door. So, we ring the bell, and Connolly goes to the door of his flat. Whoever is in the bathroom sneaks out and stabs the hypo in his neck and presses the plunger. Providing we get the dose right, he goes out like a light. The others come in and we have all the time in the world to kill him and set the scene.'

Billy nodded. 'Now that sounds like a plan.'

Archie sipped his tea and nodded appreciatively. 'It's a work in progress.'

'I like it,' said Charlie. 'But the guy inside the flat is going to be taking all the risks. If Connolly realises what's happening, one on one he's going to come out on top.'

'If he's concentrating on opening the door, and if the guy in the bathroom moves quickly enough…'. Archie shrugged. 'The trick is to have a powerful enough sedative that it knocks him out straight away. Plan B would be to wallop him with the blunt object from behind.'

'Then we don't get to see him die, and that's the whole point,' said Billy. He saw the look of surprise flash across Archie's face. 'Well it is, isn't it? That's why the bag over the head is such a great idea, we get to watch as he takes his last breath. And if we wanted to really stretch it out, we could tie him up and bring him around so that he's conscious at the end.'

'He's right,' said Charlie. 'We need some finesse. Just whacking him on the back of the head, that's amateur hour.'

'I hear you,' said Archie.

'We need to look into the sedatives we've got access to,' said Charlie. 'Maybe have a test run.'

'I don't like the sound of that.'

'It's easy enough. We just inject a small amount into one of us and see how we feel. Then extrapolate from there.' He leaned across the table. 'I think you'll have to be the one to stick it in him, squire.'

'I'm not sure about that,' said Archie, sitting back in his chair.

'Well I can't do it,' said Charlie. He put down his knife and fork and held out his hands. They trembled slightly. 'I'm okay to pick locks but I wouldn't want to depend on my hands to stick a needle in a vein.'

'And I don't have the strength,' said Billy. 'I don't know how good my lungs are going to be on the day. It won't be any good if I'm wheezing away in his bathroom, will it?'

Archie folded his arms. 'I guess you're right,' he said. 'Okay, so we've got the beginnings of a plan. We need to start gathering the PPE we'll need, and we need to nail down the tranquilliser.'

'I can do both,' said Billy. 'Sally's been getting a bit lazy when she's doling out the meds. She's supposed to make sure they swallow them in front of her but when she's rushed she leaves them to it.'

'I'll check out the work schedule so we'll know exactly what hours Connolly is working,' said Charlie. 'I'm thinking we can do it in a couple of days, right?'

'What time does he normally finish when he's on the night shift?' asked Archie.

'It varies,' said Charlie. 'Prior to covid they were on fixed shifts. There were two eight-hour day shifts and a twelve-hour night shift. But that went out of the window during covid and then when Mrs Woodhouse came in she brought in some computer scheduling system so the start and finish times are all over the place. Half of her staff are on zero-hour contracts anyway so she can do pretty much as she wants.'

'Well that's a problem right there because we need to know for sure when he leaves here.'

'It's not a problem,' said Charlie. 'There's always a schedule up on the notice board in the staff room. I can sneak in and get a look. And if there isn't, I can always sneak a look at her computer.'

Archie picked up his tea and sipped it.

'You still want to do this, right?' asked Charlie.

'Of course.'

'You seem less than enthusiastic, that's all.'

Archie shook his head. 'No, I'm good. I'm just not used to working in a group like this. Before I did all the planning.'

'Lone wolf,' said Billy.

'We're all lone wolves,' said Charlie. 'That's how serial killers operate. But for this to work, we're going to have to act as a team.'

'A pack,' said Billy.

'Exactly,' said Charlie. 'For this to work, we have to think and act like a pack. Now are you up for this. Archie? Because if you're not, you need to say so before we go any further.'

'I'm good,' said Archie. 'I want to scratch my itch as much as you do.'

Charlie fixed Archie's gaze, then smiled. 'That's what I wanted to hear,' he said.

CHAPTER 26

Archie walked out of the rear entrance and lit a cigarette. The sky overhead was a featureless gunmetal grey. It wasn't going to rain but the sun probably wasn't going to put in an appearance either. He was wearing a dark overcoat and had a red scarf wrapped around his neck. He walked by the line of mobility scooters and headed for the main entrance. A delivery van had parked in the main driveway and a woman wearing full PPE was unloading boxes of adult nappies onto a trolley. Mrs Woodhouse was standing at the rear of the van holding a clipboard. 'Going for a walk, Archie?' she asked. She was wearing a facemask and a visor, and a blue plastic apron.

'Just wanted to stretch my legs, Mrs Woodhouse.'

'I wish more of our guests felt that way,' she said. 'So many of them just sit all day. Maybe next time you could persuade Charlie and Billy to join you.'

'I will do, Mrs Woodhouse.'

'And how are you settling in?'

Archie nodded. 'I'm good, thank you.'

She gestured with her pen at his cigarette. 'You really shouldn't be smoking, you know.'

'I know, Mrs Woodhouse. I'm told it takes years off your life.' He walked away, chuckling.

He headed towards the promenade, then stopped and stood for a while smoking and looking out over the sea. After he finished his cigarette he lit another and walked north, towards the Central Pier. Just before he reached the pier he looked right and left and then jogged across the road behind a tram. He went down a side road past a large bed and breakfast with a hopeful sign saying VACANCIES and walked east for three blocks. The further he got from the sea, the shabbier the houses became and the more litter had gathered in the

147

gutters. There were dozens of silvery nitrous oxide containers around, and deflated balloons. Archie knew that nitrous oxide had become a cheap - and barely legal - high for the town's unemployed. The gas was sold, online and by dealers, in eight gram 'whippets' which were used to inflate balloons from which the gas was inhaled. The gas couldn't be breathed in direct from the whippet as when it came out of the cylinder it was close to freezing and if someone was stupid enough to try they'd end up with frostbite of the larynx.

Archie took a quick look over his shoulder. Other than a couple of stray dogs, the pavements were deserted. It was still early and Blackpool's benefits community tended to be late risers.

The grey Lexus ES was parked up ahead, the engine running. Archie walked up to the passenger door, opened it and climbed in. The driver looked across at him and sighed in exasperation. 'What the hell were you thinking, dad?' she asked.

Archie couldn't remember exactly when his daughter had decided that she was smarter than he was, but he figured it was probably when she was seven or eight years old.

'Well good morning to you, too, Jane.'

Jane had just turned forty and had been dying her hair blonde for at least a decade. Archie had never liked it blonde but had never said anything. It had been close to thirty years since she had been interested in his opinions on fashion or personal grooming. She had always respected his professional opinion on work issues, though, and he was grateful for that.

'You think it's funny? Breaking and entering?'

'To be fair now, nothing got broken.'

Jane took out her mobile phone and showed him the screen. It was one of the pictures he'd taken in Connolly's flat. 'This isn't funny, Dad.'

Archie held up his hands. 'I could hardly say no, could I?'

'You could have come up with some sort of excuse. This jeopardises everything.'

Archie eased himself forward so that he could pull his wallet from his trousers. He took out the wedding ring and showed it to her. 'He had your mum's ring. He stole them all. There was no way I was letting him keep it.'

Jane sighed. 'Why did you put it with the rest?'

'I've always had it with me. I promised her.'

'Till death do you part?'

'A promise is a promise, love.' He looked at his watch. 'We should be going.'

Jane nodded, put the car in gear, and drove down the road.

'It's still got that new car smell,' he said, putting the ring back into his wallet.

'That's because it's still new.'

'Back in my day, I couldn't have afforded a car like this. And if I could have, it would have raised all sorts of red flags.'

'Strictly speaking it's not mine for another five years,' she said. 'But the Lexus holds its value.'

'And it's a hybrid so you're saving the planet.'

'Exactly.'

'And remind me again how many child slaves mine the lithium for the batteries?'

Jane grinned and shook her head. 'I'm not letting you change the subject, dad,' she said. 'It was such a stupid thing to do. You could have jeapordised everything.'

'It was Charlie's idea.'

'Then you should have stopped him.'

'I wanted the ring back.'

'You can be so stubborn at times.'

'One of my more endearing qualities that I passed on to you. Along with a hilarious sense of humour and a love of jazz.'

'I hate jazz. I've always hated jazz.'

149

'And that was a joke.'

Jane laughed and shook her head. 'How is it in there?'

'It's like prison, but with worse food.'

'Seriously?'

Archie grimaced. 'It's pretty bad. I mean, it's bad enough for me knowing that I'm not in there for long, but for most people it's the last place they'll be. Though to be fair, a lot of them aren't really aware of their surroundings.'

She flashed him a worried look as she drove. 'Are you okay, dad?'

He shrugged. 'It's depressing, that's all.'

'You know you'll never end up in a place like that, dad.'

'You can't say that.'

'Yes I can. If ever you can't look after yourself, you can come and live with me.'

'You're keeping the house?'

Jane and her husband had recently divorced after twenty-three years of marriage. They had a son, Rick, who was at Newcastle University. 'I don't see why not. I never fell out of love with the house. Truth be told, I never stopped loving Jim either. He's the one who wanted pastures new.'

'He's an idiot,' said Archie, folding his arms.

'It's not easy living with a cop,' said Jane.

'Your mother managed okay.'

'She had her ups and downs,' said Jane. 'You just weren't there to see the downs.'

Archie didn't argue. He knew that she was right.

'I'll always have room for you, dad.' She patted him on the leg. 'But you're years away from even thinking about that.'

'Please don't tell me that eighty is the new fifty, because it really isn't.'

'We'll have you out of there soon, dad. Don't worry.'

Archie nodded. They were driving east, the tower shrinking in the distance behind them. 'We're not going to Bonny Street?' he asked.

'Bonny Street was closed years ago, dad,' she said. 'I've got us an incident room at the Blackpool Police Station HQ at Marton, next door to the big Tesco's.'

'How long's that been there?'

'Since 2018, I think. It's the West Division Police HQ, it's the base for immediate response teams, an investigations hub and there's a counter for local policing. Plus 42 custody suites, because you know how busy Blackpool can get when the stag nights are on. There are specialist teams there covering Lancaster and Morecambe, as well as Blackpool.'

It was a ten minute drive to the police HQ, a three storey modern building with an irregular white concrete structure on the outside that gave the impression that an alien had landed on it. 'What is that supposed to be?' asked Archie as they drove into the car park.

'No one is quite sure,' said Jane. 'But it cost the best part of twenty five million quid.' She parked and they climbed out.

'It's looks more like a swimming baths than a cop shop,' said Archie.

'You've got to move with the times, dad,' said Jane. They went through the main doors into a reception area. The sergeant behind the desk couldn't have been more than twenty-two, though Archie had realised it was a truism that the older you get, the younger the policemen looked. Jane signed him in and the sergeant buzzed open a door that led to a lift area, 'We'll hit the canteen first,' said Jane. 'Get you a bacon sandwich.' She pressed the button to call the lift.

'Actually I had eggs florentine for breakfast,' he said.

'Hang on, you've been telling me what a hellhole you're living in, but you had a five-star breakfast?'

'It's a long story,' said Archie.

They rode up to the third floor and Jane took him through to the canteen. It was uncomfortably modern but smelled the same as every police canteen he'd ever been in, a mix of sweat and coffee and fried food. A middle-aged woman wearing a face shield was serving a young PC and other officers sitting at the dozen or so tables scattered around. Pretty much everyone looked as if they had just left school, except for one man sitting at a table on his own. Archie's eyes widened when he realised who it was. Detective Sergeant Geordie Bacon. Or at least Retired Detective Sergeant Geordie Bacon, it must have been at least thirty years since he'd hung up his truncheon.

Geordie got to his feet as Archie walked over. He was a big man, but he had lost weight since Archie had last seen him, and he'd lost most of his hair, but there was no mistaking the large jaw with the dimple dead centre, or the amused glint in his eye. He was wearing a heavy overcoat and a Newcastle United scarf and as Archie got closer he could see that the sleeves were too long and there was slightly too much room in the shoulders.

'Jane promised me a bacon sandwich but I didn't realise this was what she had in mind,' said Archie. The two men hugged. 'Bloody hell, you're a sight for sore eyes.'

'You too,' said Geordie.

Archie looked across at Jane. She grinned. 'Surprise.'

'I haven't seen this guy for what, twenty-five years?'

'Closer to thirty,' said Geordie. 'My retirement do.'

'That's right. That was one hell of a night.'

'Took me two days to recover,' said Geordie.

'Why don't you two guys sit down and catch up while I get the coffees,' said Jane. 'My dad has already had a Michelin star breakfast, apparently, but I'll happily get you something, Geordie.'

'Sandwich, Bacon, is what we always used to ask him,' said Archie, taking off his scarf and sitting down.

'And it never got boring,' said Geordie. He sat down opposite Archie.

'Really?' asked Jane.

''What do you think?' said Geordie, his eyes twinkling.

'So what can I get you? Tea? Coffee? Sandwich, bacon?'

'A bacon roll would go down a treat, red sauce, and don't tell my doctor. Bacon is on the forbidden list, along with pretty much anything that used to give me pleasure. And coffee.' He grinned. 'Also on my banned list.'

'Tea for me, Jane,' said Archie.

'And do you want a sandwich?'

'I'm good. The Eggs Florentine did hit the spot.'

Jane was grinning and shaking her head as she walked away.

'You moved to Torquay, didn't you?' asked Archie.

Geordie nodded. 'Karen's family was there and I've always like the beach. I took up golf.'

'That's right, we bought you a set of clubs. How did that work out?'

Geordie shook his head. 'Hated the game, it turned out. What is that they say, golf spoils a perfectly good walk. I gave it a go but eventually I got rid of the clubs and got a dog instead.'

'Same here,' said Archie. 'I just couldn't get into it. And all the gear you had to trundle around with you. It was worse than pushing a trolley through Sainsbury's. I got a dog, too.' He smiled. 'So how is Karen?' Geordie's face fell and Archie realised immediately what that meant. 'Sorry, mate,' he said.

'Yeah. Cancer.'

'I'm sorry.'

'What can you do? It's cancer. The world went crazy over that bloody virus but cancer is the real killer.' He sighed. 'I miss her every day.'

'I'm sorry, mate. I wish I'd known.'

'And done what? Come to the funeral? We were in lockdown. Thirty people were allowed and we had to stay six feet apart. The kids weren't even allowed to hug me in the church.' He shook his head. 'I'll never forgive the Government for the way they handled it. They stopped her cancer treatment. The GP wouldn't visit. They gave her painkillers but at the end they weren't enough. It was unbearable, Archie. Fucking unbearable.'

Archie reached over and patted Geordie's hand. 'I'm so sorry, mate. I wish I'd been there for you.'

A tear trickled from Geordie's eye and he brushed it away. 'You wouldn't have been allowed in the house, remember?' He sniffed. 'Towards the end I wanted to call an ambulance but she said no. She knew that if they took her in she wouldn't be allowed visitors and that she'd have to die alone.' He forced a smile. 'At least we were with her, at the end.'

'The kids were there?'

Geordie nodded. 'Couldn't stop them,' he said. 'It was the week after that fuckwit Dominic Cummings drove across the country to check his eyesight, remember? And Boris stood by him. The kids said that if the PM's top adviser wasn't following the rules, why should they. Hard to argue with them. But short answer, yes, we were all there when she passed, which was a blessing.'

'And what about your health, mate? You seem fit.'

Geordie forced another smile. 'Two heart attacks and counting. But I'm still here.' He wagged a finger at Archie. 'That's what always made you such a good detective.'

'What?'

'The way you always get people to talk about themselves. You're good at that, you've always been good at that. If you need a confession and you need it quickly, call for Archie Jennings. You had the knack. The gift.'

Archie nodded. 'Well, it was different back then, wasn't it? Interviews weren't even tape-recorded, now every second is filmed. And the bad guys weren't brought up on a diet of cop shows and true crime documentaries.'

Geordie chuckled. 'Yeah, we just had The Sweeney. Get your trousers on, you're nicked.'

'To be fair, it was a bit like that, back in the day. We didn't actually fire up the Quattro, but there were plenty of Gene Hunts around.'

The two men smiled at the memories. 'It was a different world, right enough,' said Geordie. 'So what about you?'

Archie grimaced. 'Laura passed away ten years ago. Cancer. They did what they could, they always do, right? But eventually they sent her home and we had a Macmillan nurse with us. She was a God-send. At least it was pre-covid so they did all they could. It just wasn't enough.'

'Sorry, mate. And your health? You look like you're doing okay.'

'Blood pressure's up so I'm on a calcium blocker and statins. Blood sugar's too high but tablets keep it in check. Considering the whisky we drank and all the curries and bacon sandwiches we got through, I think I got off lightly. When I first had the high blood pressure, years ago, Laura put together an exercise programme for me and I've stuck with that.' He smiled. 'Sometimes when I do my press ups, I swear I can hear her urging me on.'

'How long were you married for?'

'Forty-two years.'

'Karen and I made the fifty.'

'Good for you, mate.'

Jane came over with a tray. She put it down on the table. Three coffees and two bacon rolls. She pointed at one. 'That's got the red sauce, I prefer HP.'

'Red on bacon, brown on sausage,' said Geordie. He picked up his roll and took a big bite, then sighed contentedly.

'So have you been bringing Geordie up to speed?' asked Jane as she sat down and picked up her roll.

'We were just catching up,' he said. He looked at Geordie, who was taking a second bite of his roll. 'How much did Jane tell you?'

Geordie chewed and swallowed. 'Just that you're under cover in some nursing home on the track of the Creeper.'

155

Archie sipped his tea. It was much stronger then the insipid brews he'd been given back at the home. There were two things that cops needed to function - strong tea and bacon butties - and God forbid any station that failed to come up with either. 'Well, that's pretty much it,' he said. 'You remember the McEvoy case? Lorraine McEvoy. It was just over forty years ago. Raped and strangled with a scarf. Her little girl witnessed it from upstairs. Saw the whole thing. Killer went after her but she got out of a bedroom window and jumped down onto a garden shed.'

'Yeah, I remember. Lucy, right? The little girl? Lucy McEvoy.'

'That's the one. Well, cut a long story short, last year Lucy McEvoy, who's now in her fifties, is checking her dad into the Sunnyvale Nursing Home and she recognises one of the residents as the guy who killed her mother.'

Geordie lowered his bacon roll, a look of astonishment on his face. 'After forty years?'

'I know, it sounds unlikely, but she was definite. Absolutely convinced. But sure, any jury is going to be asking the same question. After that long, how good can her memory be? The case lands on Jane's desk and she realises I was the original senior investigating officer.'

Geordie grinned. 'Are you sure this isn't just a plan to get you in a home?'

Archie laughed. 'That thought did occur to me. But it's him, Geordie. No question. He's the fucking Creeper. There's zero doubt.'

'He's confessed?'

'Can't shut him up.'

'We don't have him on tape, yet,' said Jane. 'So far we've concentrated on getting him to trust dad. But now we're ready to take it to the next stage.'

'What about Lucy?' asked Geordie. 'Has she been back to the home?'

'She booked her father in just before the coronavirus thing hit,' said Archie. 'He got through the first wave okay but he was one of the first to die during the second wave. So she wasn't allowed to visit.'

'We've shown her photographs and she's sure,' said Jane. 'And we had one of our computer experts manipulate the images to show what he would have looked like forty years ago. She's certain.'

'It'd be good to see that bastard behind bars,' said Geordie. 'Even after all this time.' He finished his bacon roll.

Jane looked at her watch. 'We'd best be going,' she said.

She took them out of the canteen and down a flight of stairs, then along a corridor to a set of double doors. She pushed them open and a buzz of conversation gradually died down as she walked in, followed by Archie and Geordie. There were more than two dozen officers in the room, most of them standing with their backs to the windows overlooking the Tesco store. A large grey table stood in the middle of the room with half a dozen chairs around it. At the far end of the room were two large whiteboards peppered with photographs, handwritten notes and newspaper cuttings.

Jane walked toward the whiteboards, nodding at several of the men. Geordie pulled out one of the chairs and sat down. The officers nearest the whiteboards moved away to give Jane room. Most of the officers were plainclothes detectives, four were uniformed constables and there were three clerical workers who had been assigned to Jane's team. They were all looking expectantly at Jane as she took up position between the two whiteboards, with Archie just behind her.

Across the top of the whiteboard on her right were the words CHARLES COOPER written in black market. Underneath was a surveillance photograph of Charlie, taken on the South Pier and below that were crime scene photographs and copies of various documents. WILLIAM WARREN was written at the top of the other board, and there was a photograph of Billy, also taken on the pier. There were more photographs and newspaper cuttings below Billy's picture.

'Right, thank you all for getting here on time,' said Jane. For anyone who's new to this, I am DI Jane Jennings and this my father, former Detective Superintendent Archie Jennings, both of Lancashire Police.' Archie raised his hand and smiled. 'The investigation we started last month has now widened, in scope and in geography, so we are now being assisted by DS Jim Miller and DC Davie Moore of the National Crime Agency.'

She gestured at two large men standing near the door, who both raised their hands. 'I'm Jim Miller,' said the taller of the two men, wearing a dark blue suit and carrying a leather briefcase. His colleague was balding with thick-lensed spectacles and had the look of an accountant. 'Moore,' he said, raising his hand.

Jane pointed at Geordie, who had spread out his legs and was leaning back in his chair. 'Also with us today is former DS Geordie Bacon who worked with my father on the original case.'

'Back when dinosaurs roamed the land,' said Geordie.

Jane grinned. 'Not quite that long ago, but the case does go back forty years and more, before a lot of you were born. Right, let me hand you over to my dad, who came out of retirement to go undercover in the nursing home where Charles Cooper and William Warren now reside.'

Jane stepped aside to let Archie take up position between the whiteboards. Archie took a few seconds to make eye contact with most of the people in the room before speaking. 'So, by way of background, DS Geordie Bacon and I were working a rape murder in Stockport, as he says, back in the days when dinosaurs roamed the land. Just over forty years ago. The victim was a single mum by the name of Lorraine McEvoy. She was raped and strangled with her own scarf in her home.'

Geordie raised his hand. 'It was her daughter's scarf. Her school uniform.'

Archie nodded. 'Right. Yes. I stand corrected. The scarf belonged to the daughter, Lucy. Lucy was seven years old at the time and she saw the whole thing. She was a very good witness, gave us a description and helped the police artist come up with a decent likeness.'

Archie pointed at a police artist's drawing of what could be a younger version of Charlie, at the bottom of a whiteboard. Next to it was a computer-generated image of a younger Charlie. The images were almost identical.

158

'Now Lucy was quite definite that the man who killed her mother was a stranger. Definitely not a family friend or relative. Lucy had never seen him before. We found that strange because there were no signs that he had forced his way in. And he'd used the girl's scarf to kill the woman, which suggested it wasn't planned. But the fact that Lucy was sure it was a stranger made us rethink what was happening and we started looking at other unsolved murders in our area, and then expanding into other areas. And that's where it got interesting.' He waved at several crime scene photographs on the board. 'We started looking at killings where there was no evidence of a break in and where any item involved in the murder was already there. We found four fairly quickly. Each was already being investigated but because of the lack of evidence of a break in, the police were looking closely at family, friends or business contacts. Unfortunately we never managed to find anything to tie the cases together and in fact my superiors doubted that we were looking for a serial killer. Geordie and I thought otherwise and we started thinking of him as the Creeper, a guy who could get in and out of homes without leaving any trace. Other than a body. By the time I retired, the investigation had pretty much petered out and they all became cold cases. I tried to convince my boss at the time that the investigation should continue, but he thought otherwise. To be honest, by the time I retired only Geordie and I were convinced we had a serial.' He looked over at Geordie, who nodded in agreement.

'The undercover operation has proved that we were right, though. Charles Cooper has admitted to me that he has been responsible for twenty-two murders.' There were several gasps from around the room. 'You heard that right,' said Archie. 'Twenty-two murders. And I have every reason to think that several of those took place after I retired.'

He pointed at the second whiteboard. 'During the course of getting close to Cooper, I came across this guy. Billy Warren. The two of them are as thick as thieves. Warren has openly boasted about killing and I have seen a collection of trophies. Eighteen locks of hair that he's taken from his victims. So between them they committed forty murders over a period of about forty years.'

Miller raised his hand. 'Archie, sorry to interrupt but do you have confessions from both?'

'They've both admitted offences to me but not on tape. I'm hoping to get them into a position where we can arrest them for conspiracy to murder. As you know that's covered by the 1977 Criminal Law Act and carries a maximum sentence of life. What I'm trying to do is to get them to…'

Jane put a hand on his shoulder. He stopped speaking and turned to look at her. 'Obviously I'll be handling operational matters, so I'll take it from here, dad,' she said.

'I was just going to explain the strategy from here on in,' said Archie.

'Well strategy is my responsibility, too,' she said. 'Let me finish addressing the troops and then we'll have a chat. Okay?'

Archie wanted to stand his ground but he didn't want to have an argument with her in front of her team so he just smiled and nodded. He stepped back and Jane turned to face the group. 'So, as my dad says, we're hoping to get a confession on tape. But even when we do have a recording, we'll need evidence to back it up. We need to contact any and all employers of Charles Cooper going back fifty years. We need timesheets and diaries, we need to know where he was and where he went, and then we can cross reference that information with the cold cases that DS Miller and DC Moore will supply. We need to know what vehicles he owned over those years and again those details need to be cross-referenced with the cold case data. We're setting up a HOLMES system which will automate the cross referencing. That should be installed later today.'

The Home Office Large Major Enquiry System could link lines of enquiry and find patterns much quicker than any human detective, but it was dependent on being fed tens of thousands of items of information and Jane had requested half a dozen civilians to assist with the input.

She moved to the side and tapped the William Warren whiteboard. 'William Warren worked as a publishing rep across the north and east of England. We need to do a similar job with him, finding out who he worked for and cross-referencing with cold cases. Unlike Cooper, Warren had a type. Blonde women. Again it's all down to cross-referencing his work sheets or diary with any unsolved rape-murders. And then we need to show his picture to any witnesses at the time, especially the computer-generated images of what they would have looked like back then. Warren has already given my father details of one of his killings - a bookshop manager by the name of Sarah McKee.' She pointed at the details of a case under the surveillance photograph of Billy. 'He abducted her by the roadside after her car broke down so we're hopeful that we will ID her quickly. And Warren claims to have buried her in woodland at the north of Norwich. We'll be starting a search in the very near future. So that's where we stand at the moment. We've a lot of hard work ahead of us but if we do this right we'll be solving dozens of murders and bringing two serial killers to justice. And providing closure to a lot of grieving families, obviously.'

Archie raised his hand. 'He also told me he used a stun gun on multiple occasions. That needs looking at.'

'Thanks, dad. Right, onwards and upwards.'

Miller had his hand up again. 'Sorry, just want to check on where we stand confession-wise. Obviously the simpler way for us to go is to have the two suspects confessing on tape.'

'Personally I think the way to go is to get them on a conspiracy charge,' said Archie. 'If we can…'

'Dad, please,' said Jane. 'Can I address Jim's question and we can talk about your ideas later?' Before he could reply she turned back to Miller. 'So far the conversations with the two suspects haven't been recorded, but we will be remedying that in the very near future. But we all know that confessions, especially those that have been recorded surreptitiously, can be problematical so we need to back them up with evidence. As it doesn't seem likely there will be forensic evidence, the timeline is the way to go.'

Miller nodded. 'Any other questions?' asked Jane, looking around the room. She was faced with shaking heads and shrugs. 'Okay, so we all know what we have to do, let's get on with it. If this all works out the way I want it to, we'll be putting forty murder cases to bed very soon.'

She threaded her way to the door. 'Sorry about that, I didn't mean to sound pushy,' said Miller.

'No, you made a good point,' said Jane. 'I'm actually on the way to get dad fixed up with a recording device as we speak. With any luck we'll have something on tape by tonight.' She gestured at Archie. 'That's down to my dad, obviously.'

Miller held out his hand and made a fist. For a second it confused Archie, then he realised that people post-covid tended to steer clear of handshakes. He made a fist and then fist-bumped. 'Hell of a job you're doing, Archie,' he said.

'Can't shut them up most of the time,' said Archie. 'They're happy to relive their exploits, they think they're talking to one of their own.'

'Well, Davie and I are here to offer whatever assistance we can, though it's clear that DI Jennings has everything in hand.'

Moore also made a fist and bumped it against Archie's. 'Your daughter is doing a great job,' he said.

'She learned from the best,' said Archie.

'Dad!'

'It was a joke, love,' said Archie, patting her on the shoulder.

'I never actually worked with my father,' Jane said to Miller.

'But I was always there for you when you needed advice,' said Archie.

Jane opened her mouth to reply but then thought better of it.

'This HOLMES is a game changer, isn't it?' said Archie. 'When I started in CID it was all notebooks and files filled with paper. HOLMES came in when? 1990?'

'1985,' said Miller. 'And then the updated version came out ten years later.'

'That's right, it was about mid way through my career. It took a lot of getting used to, I can tell you.' He chuckled. 'I remember when they said we all had to use it on every major enquiry, and they told us it was called HOLMES, after Sherlock. But the only way they could make it spell HOLMES was to have Large and Major in the title which makes no sense at all.'

'The top brass do love their acronyms,' said Jane.

'It does the job, and that's what matters,' said Moore. 'It's invaluable for an investigation like this where we have dozens of cases. HOLMES can spot in seconds what it would take a detective weeks to do if he was sifting through paper.'

'Or she,' said Jane.

Moore frowned, then his face broke into a grin as he realised what he'd said. 'Quite right,' he said. 'My apologies, ma'am.'

Jane looked at her watch. 'We have to go,' she said. She took Archie out of the room and along the corridor to a door with TECHNICAL SUPPORT on it. She knocked and went in.

Sitting at a desk dominated by three large monitors was one of the force's technicians, Sally Lawson. She looked over the top of her glasses and smiled when she saw it was Jane. 'Warrant done?' she asked.

'Signed, sealed, delivered,' she said. 'And this is my dad, former detective superintendent Archie Jennings.'

Sally got up from behind the desk and held out her hand. 'Archie, so pleased to meet you,' she said. 'Jane is always talking about you.'

Archie beamed. 'That's good to know,' he said. He made a fist and fist-bumped her. Sally was short, just over five feet, and even wearing high heels she barely reached Archie's shoulder.

'It's on the table over there, Jane,' said Sally. Sally went over to the table and Jane joined her. 'State of the art,' said Sally. 'It was developed by MI5 and they've allowed the police to have a few. So far we've had great results with it.'

Archie took off his coat and scarf and then draped them over the back of a chair. He was unbuttoning his shirt when Jane turned around and saw what he was doing. Her jaw dropped. 'What are you doing, dad?'

'I've worn wires before, Jane. I know the drill.'

Sally turned and she giggled when she saw his open shirt. 'Archie, we've moved on from a mic in your cleavage and a battery pack in your underpants.' She held up an iPhone. 'We put recording software in a phone and it acts as the recorder. It also transmits conversations in real time to our server.'

'So you can button up your shirt, dad,' said Jane.

Archie sighed and did as he was told. Sally gave him the phone. It looked like a regular iPhone.

'It's a genuine iPhone,' said Sally, as if she had read his mind. 'The only thing that is different is the software. You double click the touch sensor at the bottom to activate the recorder. It will continue to record even if you switch the phone off. Generally that's what we recommend. Activate and then switch off. That way if anyone does check the phone, it will look is if it's inactive.'

'Got it,' said Archie.

'Dad already has an iPhone so he's familiar with it,' said Jane.

'I've got a Samsung actually,' sad Archie.

'I bought you an iPhone two years ago,' said Jane.

'Yeah, I know, but I dropped it.'

'You dropped it?'

Archie nodded. 'Broke the screen. It was out of warranty and with the price they were charging to repair it, it was just cheaper to get a Samsung.'

'You should have told me, I'd have replaced it for you.'

'It's okay, the Samsung is fine.'

'But it was a present, dad.' She waved a hand at him. 'Okay, fine, it doesn't matter.'

'Really, the Samsung is fine. I don't need all the whistles and bells, anyway.'

'You can use this as your regular phone during the operation,' said Sally. 'Two phones can look suspicious, so we recommend you transfer all your numbers to this phone and use it as you would your Samsung. You can hand this to anybody and they won't find anything. As I said, it's a genuine iPhone, it's the App that does the work.'

'And try not to drop it,' said Jane. She nodded at the phone. 'So you're up to speed, right? All you have to do is set the App going, then get them talking.'

Archie grinned. 'Are you teaching me to suck eggs? I was doing undercover work while you were still being potty-trained.'

'And the way I remember it, it was mum who potty trained me.'

'I was busy, love.'

'Yeah, dad. I know.'

'But I did my fair share of nappy changing and potty-training.'

'That I don't remember.'

'You want to be careful, love, that could be early Alzheimer's kicking in.'

'Says the man who is forever wearing odd socks.'

'Who looks at socks?' he said.

'Mum used to, for a start. It used to drive her crazy.'

'Which is why I did it.' He put the phone in his pocket and then put his coat and scarf back on. 'It's been a pleasure, Sally,' he said to the technician. 'I shall do my very best not to drop it into the toilet.'

Jane took him down in the lift and outside to the car park. 'That went okay, I thought,' she said.

'You handled them well, love,' said Archie.

'They're a good team.'

'And the two guys from the NCA, you've met them before?'

'No, we only heard yesterday that they were offering assistance.'

'Just make sure they don't try and take the credit.'

'They won't, dad. This is very much my case.' She took out a pack of cigarettes and a lighter.

'Our case,' said Archie.

Jane grinned. 'Our case, yes,' she repeated. 'Don't worry, I won't be taking all the credit.'

She lit a cigarette and Archie shook his head sadly. 'I can't believe you still smoke.'

Jane shrugged. 'It's my one vice.'

'After what happened to your mum? After what it did to her.'

'Mum had cancer, dad. That doesn't mean that smoking killed her.' She blew smoke up at the sky. 'Everybody dies, dad. And look who's talking.'

Archie frowned. 'What do you mean?'

She looked at him and raised an eyebrow. 'You're still smoking.'

'I gave up ages ago.'

Jane sighed and shook her head sadly. 'You are such a bad liar.'

'Jane!'

'Dad, I'm a cop. I get lied to twenty four-seven. You think I can't spot a liar when I see one?'

'That's a terrible way to speak to your father.'

She flicked ash on the tarmac. 'Dad, I can smell the cigarette smoke on you.' She leaned towards him and sniffed his coat. 'The forensic evidence alone'll convict you.'

Archie's face fell and she smiled and hugged him with her free arm. 'I miss her too, dad.'

'I know you do, love.'

'But lots of non-smokers get cancer. And lots of smokers live long and healthy lives. Look at you. Mum was just unlucky.'

Archie nodded. 'I know,' he said quietly.

She let go of him and put the cigarette to her mouth, then had second thoughts and dropped it onto the ground and stepped on it. 'How about we both give up?' she said.

'Both of us?'

'Why not? We can both stop smoking today.'

'Love, if smoking was going to do me any damage, it would have done it already. My lungs are fine. But you, you've got your whole life ahead of you.'

'Okay. But if you want me to give up, you have to give up too.' She held out her hand.

'What?'

'Give me your cigarettes and lighter. If you're giving up, you won't need them.'

'But then you'll have my cigarettes.'

'Dad, I'm a serving police officer. If you can't trust me, who can you trust?'

'Why don't we trust each other?'

'You'll give up?'

'Sure.'

'So why are you holding on to them?'

'I give them to Charlie and Billy. They're smokers.'

'So you'll give them cigarettes and won't smoke one yourself.'

He grinned. 'That's the plan.'

She wagged a finger in his face. 'I'm not sure that I trust you,' she said.

'That's because you're a cop,' he said. He hugged her and kissed her on the top of the head. 'And a bloody good one.'

She hugged him again and then unlocked the car. They both climbed in. 'So what did you hate about my conspiracy idea?' he asked as he fastened his seat belt.

Jane didn't answer until she had started the car and was driving towards the car park exit. 'First of all, you'd be acting as an agent provocateur,' she said.

Archie grinned. 'You say that like it's a bad thing.'

Jane drove onto the road and headed west. She was a good driver, one of the best Archie had known. She was always calm and unflustered no matter what was going on around her. He had never once seen her lose her temper at the wheel or even sound her horn in anger.

'Can I ask you something?' he said as she slowed to allow a taxi to pull out in front of her.

'Sure.'

'Who taught you to drive?'

'Don't you remember?'

'Was it me?'

She laughed. 'Have you any idea how little I saw of you when I was a teenager?' she asked. She accelerated to follow the taxi.

'Yeah, I'd just been promoted,' he said. 'They were working me hard.'

'You worked yourself hard, dad. You always did. It's like you never thought you were good enough.'

'Yeah, I always pushed myself, that's true.'

'These days they'd call you an over-achiever,' she said. 'But to answer your question, mum taught me the basics in her old Volvo and then I did a few hours with BSM before my test.'

'That's right. You passed first time.'

She smiled, 'I did. And you changed the subject again, very cleverly I might add.'

'It's my super power,' said Archie.

'You didn't like me telling you that you were planning on being an agent provocateur. But that's what would happen, dad. What you're suggesting is messy. Better you get a confession on tape and we back that up with a timeline showing they had the opportunity to commit the cold case killings.'

'But that's all circumstantial. I'm offering a way of catching them in the act.'

'They killed dozens of people between them, dad. We'll get them.' She slowed to allow two cyclists to pull in front of her. They were riding two abreast as if daring anyone to try to overtake them. The were young, a man and a woman, dressed in matching blue lycra outfits and gleaming white helmets.

'I heard what you're saying, love,' said Archie. 'But even if I get a confession on tape, and even if you put together a timeline you know what juries are like. They could still walk.'

'I don't think so. You're a good witness, dad. Very credible. People believe you.'

'I've got an honest face, is that what you're saying?'

'People do tend to trust you, dad. Civilians and villains. That's why you were such a good interrogator. That's why Cooper and Warren opened up to you so easily.'

'And that's why the conspiracy idea will work. They'll trust me, right up until the time we bust them. I hear what you're saying about you putting together a case with a taped confession, but these are old guys. A good brief could claim that they've got dementia or Alzheimers and that they're talking nonsense.'

Jane shook her head. 'You're overthinking it, dad.'

The cyclists were pedalling slowly now, well under the speed limit, and were chatting to each other. By now Archie would have been pushing to overtake but Jane held back, giving them plenty of room.

'Okay, but just listen to me, okay?' said Archie. 'Like I told the guys, conspiracy to murder gets them life imprisonment. They're already planning to kill Connolly, all we have to do is wait until they try to do it.'

'We've looked into Connolly. He's got convictions for assault. He'll beat the shit out of you.'

'There'll be three of us. We can stand up to him together, if we have to. But it won't come to that. I'll record them planning the killing, you can photograph them getting the equipment, and then pick them up breaking into Connolly's flat. They can plead dementia or Alzheimers all they want, but if you catch them breaking into his flat intent on murder you've got them bang to rights.'

Jane grinned. 'We don't say "bang to rights" these days, dad. But the fact that you'll be with them throughout the planning and execution is the problem. If you get involved to that extent they'll scream entrapment.'

Archie shrugged. 'They can scream all they want. The evidence will be there which means they can be held on remand. Then we'll have plenty of time to do the legwork you're talking about. And once they're on remand you'll have their DNA and fingerprints which you can tie into the cold cases.'

Jane patted him on the leg. 'Don't take offence. You've done a great job. You went in there looking for one serial killer and you came out with two.'

'Buy one, get one free,' said Archie and they both chuckled.

'And what about Connolly?'

'Like I said, we checked him out and he's been in trouble for violence before. Mrs Woodhouse hasn't passed the video on to police. But we can pursue the sexual assault allegations once we've arrested Cooper and Warren. And the stolen goods are still in his place. Once we have a warrant we can get hold of all that. This woman you said he molested. Mrs Chalmers. What sort of witness would she make?'

Archie grimaced. 'Not great, to be honest. She can't even feed herself. That's his MO. He picks on women who are so far gone they can't stop him. We have to do something, Jane. We can't let him go on like this.'

'Let's take it one step at a time, dad. The priority at the moment is Cooper and Warren.'

'I don't want Connolly falling through the cracks,' said Archie. 'Getting Cooper and Warren is going to be a real feather in your cap.'

'And what? I'll be so busy accepting plaudits and awards that I'll forget about Connolly?'

'I didn't mean that, love. I just want Connolly to pay for what he's done.'

'It sounds like you're more upset at his offences than all the murders that Cooper and Warren committed.'

'No, of course not. But their killings are in the past, the distant past, and every day he's making life miserable for people. You don't see these old ladies crying, love. It tears at my heart. It's all I can do to stop myself walking over and punching him in the face.'

'I hear you, dad,' said Jane. 'Trust me, Mr Connolly is very much on my to-do list.'

Archie nodded and looked out of the side window. The home was in the distance. 'Can you drop me here and I'll walk the rest of the way.'

'Sure,' said Jane. She checked her mirror, indicated and pulled over. She caught Archie smiling at her. 'What?' she said.

'You're such a good driver.'

'Thank you,' she said. 'And, dad, you be careful in there, okay?'

'It's a care home, love. The clue is in the name.'

'Very funny. Don't get too blasé, dad, that's all I'm saying. These guys are serial killers, remember. They wouldn't think twice about killing you if they found out you were a cop.'

'Well they won't find out, will they?'

'Just be careful, that's all I'm saying. And if you even think something's amiss, call me and we'll pull you out.'

'I'll be fine.' He patted her on the cheek. 'It seems like only yesterday that I was the one worrying about you.'

'You didn't have much to worry about.'

'No, you were a good kid.' He looked into her eyes and smiled. 'I hope you know how proud I am of you, Jane.'

'Thanks, dad.'

'I just want you to know that.'

'I do.' She pointed a finger at his face. 'Nice change of subject. Don't forget what I said. First sign of a problem, call me.'

'I will, love,' promised Archie, opening the door.

171

CHAPTER 27

Charlie frowned down at the car. It was big and almost new by the look of it. Archie was in the front passenger seat. Charlie blew smoke out of the window. Smoking wasn't allowed in the building but Charlie couldn't be bothered going all the way down to the garden so he'd opened his window and blown the smoke out. He hadn't realised how much he had missed smoking until Archie had started offering him cigarettes, and now he was hooked again. He'd walked to a newsagents and bought his first pack for almost twenty years, and a cheap lighter. He didn't plan to go back to his old habit, but he figured a couple a day wouldn't hurt. If could survive covid, he was damn sure he could survive a few cigarettes.

He had been half way through the cigarette when the car had pulled up down the road. It was a hundred yards away, just about, but he spotted Archie almost immediately and not long afterward he recognised the woman in the driver's seat. She was the one who had delivered Archie to the home, the woman he claimed was his social worker. But Charlie had never met a social worker who drove a thirty grand motor, and the way that Archie had reached out and touched the woman's face suggested their relationship was more than professional. She couldn't have been a wife or a girlfriend, she was far too young for that, so his daughter maybe? But if she was Archie's daughter, why would he say she was his social worker. And why was he in the home in the first place if he had a daughter driving a thirty grand car?

He frowned as he blew smoke out of the window. Archie had told them that he had a son, not a daughter. A son who lived in Australia. None of this made any sense, though one thing was certain - Archie had lied to them.

As the passenger door opened, Charlie hurriedly moved away from the sill and pulled the window closed. He moved to the side, hiding behind the curtain. Archie got out of the car and bent down to look inside. He waved at the woman, then straightened up. He closed the door and stood and watched as the car did a U-turn and drove away.

When the car was out of sight, Archie took out his pack of cigarettes and lit one. As he turned to walk towards the home, Charlie stepped away from the window. He took the remains of his cigarette and flushed it down the toilet.

He grabbed his walking stick and hurried downstairs to the day room, where Billy was at their table with his dominoes. 'Any sign of Archie?' asked Billy as he opened the box and spilled the dominoes out onto the table.

'Yeah, about that,' said Charlie. He sat down, but just as he opened his mouth to speak, Archie appeared in the doorway. He waved and walked over to them.

'Hey, hey, the gang's all here,' said Archie, grabbing a chair and pulling it over.

'The wanderer returns,' said Billy.

'Anything been happening while I was away?' asked Archie.

'You missed all the action,' said Billy. 'Bono dropped by with U2 to demo his new album. Then that Megan Fox was here to show off her boob job. Then that Tom Cruise wanted to chat to us about his new movie. It's been all go. What about you?'

'I just went for a walk,' said Archie.

Billy swirled the dominoes around then they all took their tiles.

'Bollocks,' said Charlie.

Archie frowned at Charlie over the top of his tiles.

'What do you mean?' asked Archie.

Charlie wagged a finger at him 'I know exactly what you've been fucking doing.'

Charlie stared at Archie. Archie held the look, a fixed smile on his face. Billy looked at them both, wondering what the hell was going on. Eventually Charlie broke into a grin. He wagged his finger again. 'You've been practising on that crazy golf course.'

Archie laughed and slapped the table with the flat of his hand. 'I don't need to practise to beat you, mate.'

They heard a sob from across the room and they turned to see Connolly teasing one of the female residents. She was sitting in a winged armchair holding a magazine upside down. Connolly was standing behind her, flicking her ears every few seconds. She was becoming increasingly distressed and tears were running down her face. He realised that the three men were looking at him and he glared back defiantly. One by one they looked away. Charlie was the last to avert his gaze. He picked up the double-nine from his stack and placed it on the table.

'You still up for taking care of that bastard?' asked Archie.

'Yeah,' said Billy.

Charlie nodded. 'Damn right I am.'

'Then let's do it,' said Archie. 'And soon.'

CHAPTER 28

Billy rolled over and lay on his back staring at the ceiling. Something had woken him up but he couldn't hear anything. He swallowed and his mouth was dry and he was wondering whether it was worth getting out of bed to fetch a drink of water from the bathroom when he saw the dark shape by the door. As he stared at the shape he realised someone was standing there. 'What the fuck!' he exclaimed. He rolled over and switched on his bedside light. It was Charlie, leaning on his walking stick. 'Charlie, what the fuck are you doing?'

'Hush, keep the noise down,' said Charlie. He hadn't got ready for bed, he was still wearing his brown corduroy trousers and green pullover with faded leather patches on the elbows. 'And turn the fucking light off.'

'What's going on?' asked Billy, sitting up.

Charlie shuffled over to the bed and sat down on the end of it. 'He's lying,' he said quietly. He shook his head slowly. 'He's fucking lying.'

'Who's lying?' said Billy, running his hands over his head. 'What time is it?' He picked up his watch and squinted at it. His eyes refused to focus so he blinked several times until he could make out the hands on his watch. It was ten thirty.

'Archie. The fucker is up to something.'

'Up to what? Charlie, what the fuck are you talking about? Have you been mixing your meds?'

'He said he was out for a walk. He wasn't. He was in a big car with the woman who dropped him off here.'

'His social worker?'

'What sort of social worker drives a thirty grand motor?'

'Maybe she has a rich husband. Charlie, what the fuck has got into you? Are you okay? Do you want me to call for a staff member?'

'There's nothing fucking wrong with me. Archie's the problem.'

'That's why you crept into my room? Because his social worker has an expensive car?'

Charlie banged his walking stick on the floor. 'When was the last time a social worker checked up on you? This is a dumping ground. They leave us here to die and that's job done.'

'Charlie, what the fuck is your problem?'

'I don't trust him. He said his social worker was done with him. So why's he going for a ride with her? And he touched her.'

Billy frowned. 'He what?'

'He touched her face. Who touches their social worker's face? And if he was going to see his social worker, why not tell us? Why make a secret of it?' He banged his stick on the floor again. 'She isn't his social worker, that's why.'

'How did he touch her?' asked Billy.

'I don't know. He reached out and touched her cheek. Stroked her.'

'He stroked her? Stroked her how?'

'For fuck's sake, Billy. They were in a car parked in the road. I was at the window having a quick fag. They were in the car, as thick as thieves. She dropped him down the road and he walked here, like he didn't want to be seen.'

'So what are you saying? Why are you making such a big thing of this?'

'Because he's lying to us. He's been lying to us from the start, from the moment he met us. She brought him here and he said she was his social worker. That's bullshit. And we can prove it's bullshit by checking his records.'

'His records?'

'His admission form will be in his records. Come on, get up. I need your help.'

'What?'

'You heard me. Get the fuck out of bed.'

'Charlie, this is crazy…'

Charlie raised his stick and Billy could see from the look in his eyes that he was in no mood for a discussion.

'Okay, okay,' said Billy. He rolled out of bed and pulled on a pair of trousers and took a sweatshirt from his wardrobe, then sat down and put on his socks and a pair of trainers.

'For fuck's sake get a move on,' hissed Charlie.

'It's the middle of the night, I'm going as fast as I can,' said Billy. He stood up and Charlie opened the door and peered down the corridor. He waved at Billy to follow him and headed towards the stairs. They paused at the top and when they were sure that there was no one around they went down to the ground floor. There they listened again before moving on tip-toes towards Mrs Woodhouse's office.

They reached the door and Charlie opened it. They slipped inside. Charlie rushed over to the filing cabinet. 'Keep cavey,' he said.

'Keep cavey? What are you, twelve?'

'Just fucking do it.' Charlie leant his walking stick against the wall, switched on a desk lamp and pointed it towards the filing cabinet.

Billy eased the door open an inch and peered out.

Charlie ran his finger down the drawers in the filing cabinet. The third one down was labelled RESIDENTS. Charlie took out his wallet of picks and began working on the lock. His fingers were sweating and he was having trouble feeling the tumblers. Sweat was trickling off his forehead and he blinked to clear his vision.

Billy took a quick look over his shoulder just in time to see one of the picks twirl through the air and land on the carpet. Charlie cursed under his breath and knelt down slowly to pick it up, breathing heavily as he moved. He grabbed the pick, put out a hand to hold the desk, and used it to support himself as he got to his feet. 'The fucking shakes,' he said,

'You'll be fine,' whispered Billy. 'Just take it slowly.'

Charlie grunted and went back to working on the lock. Billy turned back to concentrate on the corridor. The seconds ticked by, then there was a triumphant 'yes!' from Charlie. He pulled open the drawer and rifled through the files and eventually pulled one out with the name ARCHIE JENNINGS on it. 'Here we go,' he said. He took the file over to the desk, sat in Mrs Woodhouse's high-backed chair, and opened it.

Billy eased the door closed and hurried over to stand behind Charlie. Charlie pulled out a sheet of paper that said ADMISSIONS FORM across the top. He angled the lamp to illuminate the desk better. Archie's details had been typed onto the form and there were two signatures on the bottom, Archie's and Mrs Woodhouse's. There was a space for next of kin and JANE JENNINGS had been typed in. Along with details of the relationship. He saw a single word there. DAUGHTER. Charlie tapped it. 'Look at that. Daughter. Archie is a lying bastard.'

Billy peered over his shoulder. 'Shit,' he said.

'Yeah, deep shit,' said Charlie. 'There's the proof that it wasn't a social worker who checked him in. It was his daughter.'

'But why would he lie about something like that? He said he had a son. In Australia. Why go to the trouble of lying? Why would anyone care whether he had a daughter or not.'

'Exactly. Keep watching. I'm going to check him out.' Charlie turned to Mrs Woodhouse's computer and switched it on as Billy went back to the door to keep watch.

He typed ARCHIE JENNINGS into Google. There were hundreds of hits but nothing of interest. He typed in ARCHIBALD JENNINGS but the search engine still didn't come up with anything of interest. Charlie sighed and sat back in the chair.

CHAPTER 29

Jackie Connolly burped as he opened the fridge door. It was a walk-in fridge that held food for the residents but had two shelves reserved for the staff.

'Man, that's disgusting,' said Everton, who was sitting at the kitchen table with a mug of coffee in front of him.

'Better out than in,' said Connolly. He wiped his nose with the back of his hand as he ran his eyes over the drinks and snacks. Most of them had hand-written Post-it notes on them proclaiming sovereignty. He smiled when he saw a jar of strawberry jam with Sally's name on it. He picked it up, unscrewed the top and dug in two fingers. He pulled out a strawberry and popped it into his mouth, then licked his fingers and took out another. He screwed the lid back on and put the jar on the shelf. There was a box of Mr Kipling's apple tarts at the back of one of the shelves and a Post-it note identifying it as Raja's. Connolly slid out one of the pies and bit into it, then picked up a can of Coke which also had Raja's name on it. He stepped out of the fridge and kicked the door shut.

He put the cake down on the table and popped the tab of the Coke. Everton looked up and frowned at the Post-it note. 'Isn't that Raja's?' he asked.

'Who the fuck cares?'

'I'm just saying, it's got his name on it, that's all.'

Connolly put the rest of the pie in his mouth and ripped the Post-it label off the Coke can. He screwed it up and tossed it onto the floor. 'No it doesn't.' He took a step towards Everton and glared down at him. 'Do you have a fucking problem?'

Everton met his gaze for a couple of seconds, and then looked away. 'No,' he said quietly, staring at his coffee mug.

'Yeah, that's what I thought,' said Connolly. He took a drink from the can, then burped loudly before heading out of the kitchen.

CHAPTER 30

Charlie tapped on the keyboard, then sat back and took off his glasses. He polished them on his shirt, put them back on and peered at the screen again.

'You okay?' asked Billy from the door.

'I need a stronger prescription,' said Charlie. 'My eyes are getting worse every day.'

'It's the blood pressure drugs,' said Billy. 'My eyes are fucked, too.'

'Nah, I asked them about side effects when I started on them. Dr Khan said it didn't affect your eyes. Just made your ankles swell up and maybe give you an upset stomach.'

'That'll be the same Dr Khan who said that covid would soon blow over and who then refused to come anywhere near Sunnyvale for five months? I wouldn't believe him if he told me that black was white.'

'Yeah, he's a bit of a twat,' said Charlie. He frowned and looked over at Billy. 'Wait a minute, that doesn't make sense.'

'What?'

'If he told you that black was white, he'd be wrong.'

'That's what I'm saying. The guy's always wrong.'

Charlie peered over the top of his glasses. He opened his mouth to speak but then turned back to wave at the screen. 'There are loads of people called Archibald Jennings and plenty of Archies. But none of them refer to our Archie. I've checked all the images and not one remotely looks like our guy.'

'I guess it's a common name,' said Billy. 'Try his daughter.'

Charlie nodded and tapped JANE JENNINGS into the search engine. Again there were millions of hits but those on the first page were nothing like the woman he'd seen with Archie.

He clicked the mouse to call up the images with that name and saw her almost immediately, on the fourth row of thumbnails. He clicked on the thumbnail and went through to the relevant page, and his jaw dropped. 'Fuck me,' he said.

'What?'

'Fuck me,' repeated Charlie.

Billy closed the door and hurried to the desk. Charlie's face was just inches from the screen. He sat back as Billy moved behind him. 'Detective Inspector Jane Jennings,' said Charlie, pointing at the monitor. 'His daughter is a fucking cop.'

'A cop?'

'A fucking detective. With Lancashire Police.'

Billy squinted at the screen. It was an article in the Lancashire Evening Post. The headline read 'POLICE WARNING ON PHONE SCAM' and underneath was a photograph of a middle-aged woman with dyed blonde hair in a grey suit holding up a mobile phone. 'That's the woman who brought him in that day.'

'Exactly. The one he said was his social worker. The lying bastard.'

Charlie clicked back to the search results and then clicked on another link, this one to a feature article in the Chorley Guardian. At the top of the article was a photograph of the same woman, but this time she was younger and wearing a police uniform. The headline read 'BLUE LINE RUNS IN THE FAMILY'. Charlie moved his head closer to the screen and began to read.

'Come on, let the dog see the rabbit,' said Billy, trying to push him to the side.

'It says here her father was a cop. A fucking superintendent.'

'Let me see,' said Billy.

Charlie moved to the side and pointed at the screen. 'Says she's the daughter of Detective Superintendent Archie Jennings, who is set to retire after almost forty years with the Lancashire Police.' He sat back in his chair and put his hands behind his head. 'Fuck, fuck, fuck.'

'What the fuck's going on?' asked Billy. He craned his neck to get a better look at the screen. 'Why would he tell us that she's a social worker?'

'You're missing the point, squire,' said Charlie. 'Why was he spinning us a tall tale about being a serial killing butcher when in truth he's a retired police superintendent?'

Billy's mouth fell open. 'Fuck.'

'Oh, so now realisation dawns, does it? Give me your phone.'

'You want to call somebody?'

'No you twat, I want pictures of her and her details.'

Billy took an old iPhone from his pocket and gave it to Charlie.

Charlie frowned at it. 'How do I take pictures?'

'You're a bloody Luddite, that's what you are,' said Billy. He took the phone back and set up the camera. 'Just press that thing at the bottom,' he said.

Charlie took a photograph of the screen, then photographed the contents of Archie's file. Then he entered the address of Archie's daughter into Google maps and photographed the map on the screen. She lived about fifteen miles away from the home on the outskirts of Preston.

They both heard a footfall in the corridor outside. 'Shit,' said Charlie. He shoved the phone in his pocket, groped for the lamp and switched it off. 'Hide,' he said, ducking down behind the desk.

Billy looked around the darkened room. 'Hide where?' he whispered.

'Anywhere.'

Billy couldn't see anywhere to hide so he rushed over to the door. Just as he flattened himself against the wall, the door opened. 'Who's in here?' barked a voice. It was a Northern Irish accent. Connolly.

Connolly stepped into the room, then groped for the light switch. Billy held his breath. He was behind the door and providing Connolly stayed where he was, he wouldn't be spotted.

Connolly moved towards the desk. 'Come on, out with you. I heard you talking, I know you're in here. So stop fucking about.' He was holding a can of Coke and he drank some and then burped loudly. He took a step forward, then stopped again. 'I can fucking see you there behind the desk, now stand up or I'll fucking give you what for.'

Charlie slowly got to his feet, using the desk as leverage.

'Charlie fucking Cooper, I might have fucking known,' said Connolly. 'What the fuck are you doing? Have you been playing around with Mrs Woodhouse's computer.' His frown deepened. 'Is that about that video you showed Mrs Woodhouse? You and I need to have a chat about that. What the fuck did you think, that you'd get me into trouble?' He sneered at Charlie. 'I didn't float up the Lagan in a bubble, you stupid fucker. I can twist that bitch around my little finger any way I want to. Trust me, your little scheme is going to come back and bite you in the arse, big time.' He spotted the open file on the desk. 'And what the fuck is that? Have you been going through her files? What the fuck are you up to, you stupid old fart?'

Billy looked around for something he could use to hit Connolly but the only thing within reach was a large potted plant. He bent down slowly and picked it up.

'What, cat got your tongue, Charlie?' said Connolly. 'Looks like this might be a case for the cops. Unless you want to come to an arrangement?'

'An arrangement?' repeated Charlie. 'What do you want?'

Connolly laughed. 'What have you got? You old guys always have something of value tucked away.'

He drained his Coke can, crumpled it with one hand and tossed it into a waste paper bin. He grinned at Charlie and burped again.

Billy came up behind him and smashed the plant pot against the back of Connolly's head. Connolly slumped to the ground like a dead weight. The plant pot shattered and soil and pieces of broken pottery littered the carpet.

Charlie hurried around the desk. 'Get the door. Hurry.'

Billy took a quick look to make sure there was no-one else in the corridor, then closed the door.

Charlie knelt down by the side of the unconscious Connolly and began taking off the man's belt.

'What are you doing?' asked Billy.

'What does it look like I'm doing?' said Charlie. He pulled out the belt and wrapped it around Connolly's neck.

'Charlie!' protested Billy. 'You can't do that.'

Charlie threaded the belt through the buckle and pulled it tight. 'We've no choice. Archie is a fucking cop. He knows everything. We're up shit creek no matter what happens. We might as well go out in a blaze of glory.'

Billy considered what Charlie had said, and then realised that he was right. He walked over and kicked Connolly in the side, hard. 'Bastard!' he hissed. He kicked Connolly again, even harder this time. 'Fucking bastard!'

Charlie pulled the belt tighter still and put his knee in the small of Connolly's back. Connolly's eyes flickered open and then his body began to buck in an attempt to throw Charlie off.

'Help me,' grunted Charlie as he fought to keep a grip on the belt.

Billy knelt on Connolly's legs.

Connolly began to rock from side to side, then suddenly he grabbed a handful of Charlie's shirt and pulled. Charlie lost his balance and Connolly kicked out, managing to dislodge Billy.

'Hold him down,' said Charlie, fighting to keep his grip on the belt. He grabbed Connolly with his knees and leaned back as he tugged on the belt. Connolly's face had gone red and his eyes were bulging. 'Come on you bastard, die!' hissed Charlie.

Connolly managed to get both his hands on the floor in front of him and he started to push himself up. Charlie leaned forward to press down on him but that meant the belt loosened around Connolly's neck and he took in a lungful of air. Charlie pulled back and Connolly kicked out with his legs and managed to dislodge Billy who fell sideways and hit his head against the wall. Connolly roared in triumph. He put his hands on the floor again and pushed himself up. This time Charlie leaned backwards, keeping the pressure on the belt. Connolly got onto all fours and began to crawl to the desk with Charlie on his back.

'Billy, help me!' shouted Charlie.

There was a coat rack to the left of the door. Billy pushed himself to his feet and grabbed it, then started hitting Connolly about the legs with it. Connolly ignored the blows and continued to crawl until he reached the desk, then he put his hands on it and began to get to his feet.

Billy swung the coatrack against Connolly's knee. He grunted but continued to stand up. Charlie slid off Connolly's back, gripping the belt with both hands. His feet hit the ground just as Billy was swinging the coat-rack again and it thudded against Charlie's leg. Charlie yelped.

'Sorry,' said Billy. He raised the coatrack again but Charlie had started to push himself back. Charlie crashed into Billy and the three men staggered back. Billy hit the door with a loud thump and the coat-rack fell from his grasp. Connolly whirled around and swung Charlie with him. Charlie banged into a coffee table and knocked it sideways, then Connolly threw himself backwards and smashed Charlie into a wall. Charlie let go of the belt and Connolly turned around, bellowing in triumph. Charlie went down on one knee, gasping for breath.

'You fucking bastard!' Connolly shouted, drawing back his fist.

Billy ran forward and grabbed the belt with both hands. He pulled it hard and Connolly's head snapped back with an audible crack. Billy kept the pressure on and Connolly had no choice but to stumble backwards, his hands clawing at his throat.

Mrs Woodhouse's badminton kit was on a chair next to Charlie and a racket was sticking out. Charlie seized it and started hitting Connolly in the stomach with it. The racket made a satisfying thudding sound but didn't seem to be doing any damage. Connolly's mouth was open as he gasped for breath so Charlie turned the racket around and thrust the handle between Connolly's teeth. Connolly grunted and grabbed the racket. He twisted it from Charlie's grasp and lashed out, dealing Charlie a glancing blow across the face. Charlie's glasses flew off and he staggered back.

'We need to get him on the floor,' gasped Billy, still hanging onto the belt. Connolly turned, trying to get at Billy, but Billy moved with him, keeping the pressure on the belt. Connolly's eyes were bulging now and spittle was bubbling from between his lips. 'Come on!' shouted Billy. 'I need some help here!'

Charlie grabbed a chair and swung it at Connolly's legs. Connolly grunted and fell back but Billy kept the pressure on the belt.

'Again!' shouted Billy.

Billy crashed the chair into Connolly's legs a second time and this time they buckled and he fell to his knees. Charlie kicked him in the back and Connolly slumped forward until the belt jerked him back. Billy moved forward and pushed Connolly down.

Connolly rolled onto his back but before he could move Billy planted his right foot in the middle of his chest and pulled the belt tight.

Connolly clawed at Billy's legs but he was rapidly losing his strength.

'Help me!' shouted Billy. 'The bastard won't die.'

Charlie looked around for something to use as a weapon. He saw the fish tank and went over to it. He picked it up. It was heavy but he could manage it. He lifted it off the cabinet with a grunt and carried it over to Connolly.

'Are you fucking kidding me?' shouted Billy.

Charlie began to pour water over Connolly's face. Connolly spluttered and coughed, turning his head from side to side as he tried to avoid the torrent of water. A goldfish flopped out, smacked against Connolly's cheek and rolled onto the carpet. Another fish fell out, then a plastic galleon. The water was cascading over Connolly's face and he was gasping for breath.

Billy was pulling with all his might and Connolly's lips were starting to turn blue. He was still trying to claw at Billy's legs but there was almost no strength to his movements. Charlie tipped out the last of the water and stared down at Connolly. Connolly's eyes were wide and staring but with life still in them.

'Pull harder!' said Charlie.

'I'm pulling as hard as I can, the fucker won't die!'

Connolly began kicking out with his legs but Billy's foot kept his chest pinned to the floor.

'He'll die, just keep the pressure on.'

'I'm knackered, Charlie.'

'I'll help you.'

'Hit him. Hit him with something.'

Connolly was groaning and his chest was heaving but they had both seen death up close and knew that there was still plenty of life left in the man.

Charlie looked around for something to use to hit Connolly.

'The tank, man! Use the fucking tank.'

Charlie looked at the tank and then at Billy.

'Go on! Let him have it!'

Charlie turned the tank so that the narrow end was pointing down. He raised it in the air and then smashed it on Connolly's head. The nose splattered against the glass just before it shattered, then the metal sides cut through the flesh. The side panels stayed intact but glass tinkled around Connolly's bleeding face as Charlie raised the tank again. He brought it down with more force this time and the face crumpled into a bloody mess as two of the side panels cracked and broke. Sand erupted from the tank and more glass fell around Connolly's head as his blood soaked into the wet carpet.

'Again!' said Billy.

Charlie grunted, lifted the tank and smashed it against Connolly's skull. The metal frame hit his forehead and it cracked open with the sound of wood splintering, revealing greyish beige brain matter. Charlie took a step back, his chest heaving. He let go of the tank and it clattered to the floor, scattering more sand and broken glass on the carpet.

Connolly's hands fell to his sides. Charlie staggered back until he was against a wall, then he slid down it until his knees were up against his chest.

Billy kept the pressure on the belt even though Connolly's chest had stopped moving, but eventually he let go. The belt fell onto Connolly's chest. Billy put his hands on his hips and looked over at Charlie. They were both bathed in sweat and gasping for breath.

It was more than a minute before Charlie spoke. 'How was it for you?' he asked.

'It was the dog's bollocks.' Billy wiped his face with his hand and it came away wet. 'It was messy. But yeah, it felt good. What do we do now?'

Charlie shrugged. 'What can we do? We're fucked.'

'We could hide the body.'

Charlie laughed, but the sound came out as a savage bark. 'And clean the carpet? And replace the fish tank? And the fish? Nah, Billy, we're fucked. Archie's a cop. Or a retired cop. And his daughter's a detective. We've already told him enough to see us put away for the rest of our lives. Not that either of us have got long, but that's not the point.' He rested the back of his head against the wall and sighed. 'This is not what I'd planned.'

'Neither of us planned this, Charlie, but now we've got to deal with things the way they are, not the way we want them to be. So what are we going to do?'

Charlie took his cigarettes out and lit one. He blew smoke as he stared at Connolly's body. 'Go out in a blaze of glory maybe.'

'Can I have one?' asked Billy.

'Sure,' said Charlie. He held out his pack and Billy walked over and took one. Billy bent down as Charlie lit it for him. Then Charlie held out his hand and Billy helped him to his feet. Charlie went over to Connolly and knelt down next to him, grunting with the exertion. He started going through his pockets.

'What are you looking for?' Billy asked.

'His car keys.'

CHAPTER 31

Archie opened his eyes and he blinked, trying to focus. Someone had switched on the light. There were two figures in the room, and it took him several seconds of blinking to realise that it was Charlie and Billy. 'What the fuck, guys?' he said. 'What time is it?'

'Time you get what's coming to you, arsehole,' said Charlie. He handed his walking stick to Billy and picked up Archie's bathrobe off the armchair.

'Guys, seriously,' said Archie, sitting up. 'What's going on?'

Billy swung the stick at Archie's head and Archie threw up his hand to block it. The stick hit his forearm and he grunted in pain. He tried to grab the stick but Billy moved away, holding it with both hands like a baseball bat.

Charlie pulled the belt from the robe and wrapped both ends around his hands.

Billy took another swing at Archie and he rolled across the bed and stood up. 'What the fuck, guys?'

Billy slapped the bed with the stick. 'You bastard,' he said. 'We fucking trusted you. We let you into our group, we shared, we confided in you. And all the time you were lying to us.'

Charlie took a step forward, holding the belt in front of him. 'We know who you are, you bastard,' he said. 'And we know what you're up to.'

Archie put up his hands defensively. 'What the fuck are you talking about?'

'Butcher my arse,' said Charlie. 'You were a cop. And that so-called social worker is your fucking daughter. And she's a cop, too.'

'Guys…' said Archie, but his words were cut short when Billy jabbed the stick in his stomach. The breath exploded from his body and he bent double.

Charlie moved quickly, stepping forward and winding the belt around Archie's neck. Archie clutched at it with his fingers but Charlie pulled back, keeping him off balance. Archie tried to speak but the belt was too tight and all he could do was grunt. Billy went around to face Archie and drew back the stick to hit him in the stomach. Archie lashed out with his foot. He caught Billy in the stomach and pushed him back. The stick fell from Billy's hands and clattered on the floor as he staggered back and collided with the dressing table.

'You bastard!' shouted Billy. He bent down to pick up the stick but Archie kicked out and hit him in the stomach. Billy took a step back and then lost his balance and went down on one knee, gasping for breath.

Charlie pulled tighter on the belt and Archie's chest heaved as he fought to breathe. Archie tried to twist around but Charlie kept the pressure on. Archie could hear the blood pounding in his ears and felt the strength draining from his legs. He feigned a turn to the left but then twisted to the right and the manoeuvre caught Charlie by surprise. Archie continued to move to the right and Charlie scrabbled to keep his balance. The pressure eased on the belt and Archie was able to suck in air.

Billy had picked up the walking stick again and he jabbed it at Archie's stomach. Archie kicked out but his legs had gone weak and he couldn't even connect with Bill.

'You bastard!' said Billy. He lashed out with the stick and hit Archie below the knee. Archie's yell was cut short by the belt tightening. He could feel Charlie's hot breath on his neck and he pushed back, hoping to get him off balance again.

They crashed back into the wardrobe but the belt stayed tight across Archie's neck. Archie twisted around and tried to push Charlie back towards the bed, figuring that if he could throw himself on top of the man he might wind him enough to make him lose his grip.

Charlie resisted and Billy came over and tossed the stick on the bed. 'Let me help,' he said, grabbing one end of the belt from Charlie.

He quickly looped it around Archie's neck a second time before pulling it tight. With Charlie on one end and Billy at the other, the belt got tighter and tighter. Everything started to go black and the blood was pounding so hard that Archie felt as if his head was going to explode. He clawed at the belt but there was nothing he could do and as the strength faded from his legs he sank to his knees.

'We've got the bastard now, just a few more seconds,' gasped Charlie.

They were the last words Archie heard before everything went black.

CHAPTER 32

Everton wiped the tissue through the crack of Tommy's backside. Tommy was leaning forwards to give Everton room to work. Even through his N95 face-mask the smell was pretty awful but Everton had smelled worse and Tommy was a nice enough guy.

Tommy farted for the third time. 'Better out than in,' he laughed.

'Yeah, I'm not sure I agree with that, Tommy,' said Everton.

'I'm sorry,' said Tommy. 'I just can't reach, you know? My arm just locks up.'

'No need to apologise, Tommy. At least you use the toilet, it's a hell of a lot more work if you soil the sheets.'

Tommy gritted his teeth and farted again. 'All done,' he said.

'Good to know,' said Everton.

They both heard a loud bang from one of the rooms down the corridor. Everton frowned. Mrs Grainger used to fall out of bed but they had switched her into a hospital model with guards on either side which had worked a treat. Another of the residents on the ground floor had an epilepsy problem but his seizures tended to create a drumming thudding sound rather an a single bang.

Everton dropped the soiled tissue in the toilet and pressed the button on top of the cistern, then he helped Tommy to stand and pull up his pyjama bottoms.

Another bang echoed down the corridor as Everton walked Tommy back his bed. Tommy sat down, then slowly swung his legs onto the bed before lying down and pulling the duvet over him. Everton let him do it himself, it was always best to have the residents do as much as they could by themselves.

'Good to go, Tommy?'

'What about a goodnight kiss?' said Tommy. 'I promise not to slip you the tongue.'

'That's an image I'll take with me to my grave,' said Everton. He went back to the bathroom, stripped off his latex gloves and dropped them into the hazardous waste bin under the sink and put on a fresh pair. He went back into the bedroom, switched off the light and slipped into the corridor.

He stood still listening but he couldn't hear anything out of the ordinary. The room opposite Tommy's was empty, the one to the left was occupied by a Mrs Dawson but she was as good as gold and went out like a light every night at ten on the dot. Everton walked along the corridor and by Mrs Dawson's room. The next room was Archie's and Everton realised there was a strip of light under the door. Everton knocked on the door and twisted the handle. As he pushed open the door he gasped and for a second he couldn't believe what he was seeing. Charlie and Billy were on top of Archie, pulling at a piece of white cloth around his neck. Charlie looked up at Everton., His eyes were filled with rage and his lip was curled back in a snarl. He was holding one end of the cloth strip on both hands and he was pulling it tight. Billy had the other end and he too glared at Everton.

'What the fuck's going on?' Everton asked, taking a step into the room. The two men looked at each other, then back at Everton. He took another step towards them. 'You two guys need to get up and back away from Archie.'

Charlie did as he was told. He stood up and scrambled across the room to pick up his walking stick.

'What the fuck are you playing at?' asked Everton, hurrying over to the prostrate Archie. 'Have you killed him?'

Billy stood up and went over to Charlie. Charlie was holding the walking stick, still breathing heavily. 'What do we do?' Billy asked Charlie.

Everton answered the question for him. 'You're going to stay right there,' he said. 'Don't either of you move a muscle.'

He had to walk past them to get to Archie and he stared menacingly at them, daring them to do anything but obey him.

Archie was lying face down on the carpet and he wasn't moving. Everton rolled him over. His eyes were closed, his mouth was open and his chest wasn't moving. There were livid red marks around his throat. Everton knelt down and felt for a pulse in his neck. He glared up at Charlie and Billy. 'What the fuck was this about? You've killed him.'

Charlie waved his walking stick. 'Serves the fucker right!' he said.

'What the fuck has got into you two?' Everton hissed.

Charlie looked at Billy. 'Come on, let's go,' he said.

'You're not going anywhere,' said Everton.

The two men headed for the door. Everton was just about to get to his feet to stop them when he felt a faint throb at his fingertips, He looked down at Archie but there were no signs of life. He put his hands together and started doing chest compressions. When Everton had trained on chest compressions his instructor had been gay and had suggested using Abba's Dancing Queen as the tune to keep the pace. Once the course was over Everton had discovered that Staying Alive by the Bee Gees was the more traditional choice and that was what was running through his mind as he pounded Archie's chest.

Charlie and Billy slipped out of the door. 'Bastards!' shouted Everton. He looked down at Archie. He didn't appear to be breathing and there was a bluish tinge to his lips. 'Don't you fucking die on me, Archie,' Everton muttered. He stopped the chest compressions and opened Archie's airway, lifting up the chin and tilting back his head. He put his ear close to Archie's mouth but heard and felt nothing. He sat back on his heels. He was going to have to try mouth-to-mouth but even pre-covid he had been told never to do it without a CPR mask and the nearest one was in the staff room. 'Fuck it,' said Everton. He pulled off his N95 mask, licked his lips nervously, then covered Archie's mouth with his own. He used his right hand to pinch Archie's nose closed, and blew in for a second, enough to make the chest move. He did a second breath, then restarted the chest compressions. After thirty chest compressions he switched back to mouth-to-mouth, but just as he started the second breath Archie shuddered and coughed. Everton sat back on his heels and started to laugh uncontrollably.

Archie's eyes fluttered open and he squinted up at Everton. 'What's so funny?' he asked, and that made Everton laugh even harder.

CHAPTER 33

Billy undid the steering wheel lock and tossed it onto the back seat. 'You sure you want me to drive?' he asked Charlie, who was in the passenger seat.

'My night vision went years ago,' said Charlie.

Billy put the key in the ignition and started the engine. 'I'm not sure mine is any better,' he said.

'Just drive,' said Charlie, pointing at the car park exit.

Billy drove out. 'Head east, away from the promenade,' said Charlie.

'What are we going to do, Charlie?' Billy asked.

'We're going to keep going. We're like fucking sharks now, if we stop, we die.'

Billy flashed him a sideways look. 'Keep going?"'

'Yeah. We've moved up in the world. We've gone from serial killers to spree killers.'

Billy laughed. 'I guess we have. So we're going out in a blaze of glory?'

'It's the only way to go,' said Charlie, beating a tattoo on the dashboard with his palms. 'Top of the world, ma!'

CHAPTER 34

Everton handed Archie a glass of water. Archie was sitting on his bed. He drank the water greedily. Everton took a step back and folded his arms. 'What's this all about, Archie?'

'It's a long story. Where did they go?'

'I don't know. What do you mean, it's a long story? They were trying to kill you, Archie.'

Archie rubbed his throat gingerly. 'I was lucky you came along.'

'We need to call the cops.'

'I am the cops, Everton. Or at least, I used to be a cop.'

'Bullshit,' said Everton. 'You used to be a butcher.'

Archie shook his head. 'I was a police superintendent.'

'Why did you lie?'

'Like I said, it's a long story.'

'Whatever, I need to get Jackie. He's in charge at night, everything has to go through him.'

'Okay, wait, let me get dressed.' Archie pulled on a pair of trousers and a pullover, then his socks and shoes, while Everton waited impatiently, switching his weight from foot to foot. ''Everton, mate, I'm doing this as fast as I can,' said Archie. 'At my age, getting a sock on in less than a minute is like breaking the sound barrier.' He picked up his phone and nodded at Everton. 'Okay, let's go find him.'

They walked along to the kitchen but there was no sign of Connolly. 'You sure he's not abusing one of the clients?' asked Archie.

Everton frowned. 'Why would you say that?'

'You know that he does, right? That's presumably why he prefers the night shift.'

'And you think I should do something about it?'

'Somebody should,' said Archie.

'Look, Archie, he's tight with Mrs Woodhouse. She won't do anything.'

'And you don't want to lose your job, is that it?'

'You're retired and, if you were a cop, then you'll be on a decent pension. You don't know how tough it is out there, so don't start lecturing me on what I should or shouldn't do. At the moment the task at hand is to find Connolly and then we can call the police.'

'Okay, okay,' said Archie. 'I was just thinking that if he's slipped into the rooms of one the residents then he's going to be hard to find.'

Everton's eyes narrowed when he saw the strip of light oozing out from under the door to Mrs Woodhouse's office. 'What's going on there?' he said. He hurried down the corridor and threw open the door. He cursed and took half a step back.

'What is it?' asked Archie. He came up behind Everton and looked around him, then gasped when he saw the carnage. Connolly's face had been smashed beyond recognition and there was blood, broken glass and sand all over the body. A shattered fish tank lay on the floor, clearly the murder weapon, though there was also a belt around Connolly's neck.

Everton hurried over to Connolly but as he knelt down it was a clear that the man was beyond help. 'What the fuck is going on tonight?' asked Everton.

'I'm going to call the police,' said Archie, pulling out his phone. He walked around the desk and his jaw dropped when he saw what was on the screen.

Everton saw his reaction. 'What's wrong?'

Archie pointed at the monitor. 'That's my daughter. That's Jane.'

Everton stood up and went over to look at the screen. 'She's a cop?'

Archie nodded. His jaw tensed when he saw the open file on the desk. 'And they've got her address,' he said.

CHAPTER 35

Charlie looked down at his phone. The map he had photographed filled the screen. 'Next left,' he said. They had been driving for just over twenty minutes and were on the outskirts of Preston.

Billy indicated and made the turn, the headlights of the Polo illuminating a line of near-identical modern semi-detached houses.

'There it is,' said Charlie, pointing ahead. 'That's the car I saw outside Sunnyvale.'

Billy peered through the windshield at the grey Lexus parked in the driveway of one of the houses. 'What do you want to do?' he asked.

'Just drive by, let's see how the land lies. Not too slowly.'

'Gotcha,' said Billy.

They drove by and both men looked through the side window. The lights were on in the front downstairs room. 'She's home,' whispered Charlie. 'The bitch is home.'

CHAPTER 36

Jane was lying on her sofa with a glass of red wine resting on her stomach as she flicked through her Netflix menu with the remote. There was nothing she wanted to watch and it felt as if over the past few weeks she had spent more time looking for something to watch than actually watching. She had disconnected her aerial and stopped paying for her TV licence a year earlier but was now starting to regret her decision.

She switched off the TV, lifted up her glass and swung her stockinged feet off the sofa. 'Time for a bath,' she said to Tippy, her black and white cat who was curled up on the armchair. Tippy stretched out her front paws, yawned, and went back to sleep.

Jane topped up her glass with wine and headed for the stairs. The previous day she had bought two new vanilla scented candles and some lavender and vanilla bath salts that she was eager to try out. She put her wine glass on the shelf by the taps and lit the two candles with her lighter. A sweet vanilla fragrance filled the room.

She turned on the taps and poured a large measure of bath salts into the water, then added a couple of capfuls of Radox Muscle Soak. A mass of foam began to fill the bath.

Downstairs, her phone began to buzz, but she couldn't hear it over the sound of the running water.

CHAPTER 37

The call went through and Archie heard Jane's voice. He started to speak but realised almost immediately that he was talking to her voicemail. 'This is Jane Jennings, I can't get to the phone so leave me a message or send me a text.' Archie paced up and down as he waited for the beep. Everton was standing by the door, his arms folded. Eventually he heard the beep. 'Jane, it's dad. Call me as soon as you get this. It's urgent. Call me.' He ended the call and looked over at Everton. 'Answer machine,' he said.

'You need to call the cops,' said Everton. 'This is some mixed up shit.'

Archie nodded. 'I know,' he said.

'What are you thinking? That Charlie and Billy are after your daughter.'

Archie nodded again. That was exactly what he was thinking. He tapped out nine-nine-nine.

CHAPTER 38

Jane sighed and slid down into the warm, fragrant water. She sipped her wine and smiled to herself. She'd had a hard day, not physically demanding but mentally challenging with literally hundreds of decisions to be taken as they worked to put together a case against Cooper and Warren. The HOLMES terminals had been installed and the civilian operators had begun keying in the relevant data. Jane could feel her pulse begin to quicken as she thought about the case, and she forced herself to relax. She stretched out and took a long sip of wine. What she really wanted was a cigarette but she had promised her dad she wouldn't smoke and she intended to stick to that.

She smiled at the memory of the way her dad had started unbuttoning his shirt in the police station. He had been a great copper in his day, but the world had moved on. Back in his day policing had been about thief-taking, catching villains and putting them away. But twenty-first century policing was much more political, more budget-conscious and under more scrutiny than it had been in her dad's day. Everyone carried a mobile phone and a misunderstanding or indiscretion could go viral within hours, ending a career or at least blighting it. Police forces were now services, and policing was more about keeping the community happy than about catching villains. She sipped her wine. In many ways her dad had been lucky. Back in his day cops could play hunches, they could even bend the rules, it was results that mattered and her dad had been one of the best when it came to results. But now every interview was recorded, sound and vision, and the HOLMES system monitored and assessed every step of an investigation. The result of an investigation often now seemed less important than how an enquiry was conducted, that all the boxes were ticked and health and safety taken into consideration every step of the way. Her dad had been a detective superintendent, and he'd been a damn good one. But now promotions more often than not were a matter of filling quotas and Jane knew that she had personally missed out on at least two promotions because she had been the wrong colour and sexual persuasion. And all the signs were that it was getting worse, not better. She was fairly sure that by the time she reached the end of her career, all the country's top cops would all be gay, black, Asian or disabled.

She sipped her wine and took a deep breath, then closed her eyes and tried to clear her mind.

CHAPTER 39

The wheels of the police car screeched as they took the corner and Archie was thrown to the side. He had asked the officers to step on it but not to use the blues and twos. If Cooper and Warren were at Jane's he didn't want them to know that the police were on the way.

He tried calling her again but like every other call it went through to voicemail.

'No joy, sir?' asked the cop in the front passenger seat. PC Ahmed had a neatly-trimmed beard but even with the facial hair didn't look as if he was long out of his teens. Archie figured the PC had joined the cops twenty years after Archie had retired. In fact there was a reasonable chance that PC Ahmed hadn't even been born when Archie handed in his warrant card.

'Voicemail,' said Archie, looking out of the side window as the houses flashed by.

'We're about eight minutes away, sir,' said PC Ahmed.

Archie had called nine nine nine and asked for a car to go straight to Jane's house but the woman on the end of the line had point blank refused and insisted that the officers would have to speak to him first. She didn't care that he was a retired superintendent, she didn't care who he knew, she had a procedure to follow and that procedure meant the police had to talk to him first. As soon as she had ended the nine-nine-nine call, Archie phoned two senior police officers at home but both had retired and while they promised to make some calls, he knew that time was running out.

When the patrol car had eventually turned up, the two constables had listened as Archie tersely told them what had happened and that they needed to get to Jane's house as soon as possible. The driver, who was a woman a few years older than PC Ahmed, knew who Jane was, which was a plus, but she was also a stickler for procedure which meant that she insisted on seeing the body. Everton had confirmed everything that Archie told them, but that wasn't good enough so Archie and Everton took them inside the building and along to Mrs Woodhouse's office. Things started to move quickly once they saw Connolly's body. They called into their control room, explained the situation and were given permission to drive Archie to Jane's house. Archie asked them to send an armed response unit but was told that there were only two units and both were out on firearms calls.

Everton had stayed with the body with instructions not to let anyone into the room.

'These two men, they want to kill DI Jennings?' asked the driver. She was driving at just above the speed limit, occasionally flashing her headlights before stamping on the accelerator to overtake.

'I think so,' said Archie. 'They tried to kill me and they have my daughter's address.'

'And they live in an old folks home?''

'Yes.'

'So they're what, in their eighties?' said PC Ahmed. 'And they did that to the guy in the office?'

'They're old but they're dangerous,' said Archie. 'Did you ever hear of The Creeper?'

'That's a movie, right?' said the driver.

'No, it's a serial killer. Active before you two were born. One of those guys is The Creeper and he killed twenty-two people. The other guy murdered eighteen women. So old or not they are very dangerous men.'

He tried calling Jane again but voicemail kicked in almost immediately.

CHAPTER 40

Jane drank the last of her wine, sat up and pulled out the bath plug. She stood up, put the empty glass on the shelf by the taps and used a shower attachment to rinse off the suds before stepping out of the tub and grabbing a fluffy white towel. She towelled herself dry and then pulled on a white bathrobe. She used another smaller towel to wrap around her head, picked up the wine glass and padded downstairs.

She went through to the sitting room and poured herself more wine. She frowned as she looked down at her phone and saw that she had seven missed calls, She bent down and picked up the phone. It had been her dad. 'Now what?' she sighed.

She took a long drink of wine, put the glass on the coffee table, and pressed the button to return the call. He answered almost immediately. 'Jane! Thank God!'

'Dad, what's wrong?'

'Where are you?'

'I'm at home. I just got out of the bath. '

'Jane, listen to me. Cooper and Warren know who you are and where you live.'

Jane's head swam. 'What? How?'

'They just do. And they've taken a car. They killed Connolly and they tried to kill me.'

Jane put her hand on her forehead. She was finding it difficult to process what she was being told. 'Dad, none of this makes any sense. You mean Jackie Connolly? At the home? The abusive care-worker?'

'They battered him to death in Mrs Woodhouse's office.'

'Where are you, dad?'

'I'm in a patrol car heading your way.'

'Why?'

'Because they've got your address. They got it from the admission form. They know where you live, Jane.'

Jane sighed. 'Dad, I'm inside and the door's locked. And I have an alarm. Safe as houses. Literally.' She bent down and picked up her glass.

'Cooper was a locksmith, Jane. Barricade yourself in a room. Any room. And wait for us.'

'I think you're over-reacting, dad.' She took another sip of wine,

'Just do as you're told.'

Jane laughed. 'Dad, I'm not twelve years old.'

'I know. Sorry. Just get to a safe place and wait for us.' She heard him talk to someone else in the car, then he was back on the line. 'We're about eight minutes away,' he said.

'Okay, okay. I'll put the kettle on.'

'Jane, you heard what I said. Lock yourself in a room. Just do it. And stay on....'

'Yes, dad, no dad, three bags full, dad,' she said, cutting him off. She put the phone back on the coffee table and took another sip from her glass. As she turned, she realised that someone was standing in the doorway. Billy Warren. And he was holding a knife. A knife that she had last seen in her knife block in the kitchen.

She gasped and threw her glass at him. It smashed into the wall to his left and wine splattered over the floor. Bits of glass tinkled onto the varnished bare boards. He sneered. 'You throw like a fucking girl,' he said.

'That's because I am a fucking girl,' said Jane. She picked up the wine bottle and pretended to throw it at Billy, and grinned when he ducked. She upended the bottle and held it by the neck, swinging it like a club.

'Feisty, huh?' said Billy.

'You don't have to do this, Billy.'

He grinned savagely. 'Do you have any idea how many times I've heard that over the years?'

'Things have changed. You're older. Not wiser, but older. And I'm not prepared to be a victim.'

'You don't get to choose. There's the hunter and there's the prey. We both have our roles.' He stepped towards her, keeping the knife pointed at her stomach.

'I'm a police officer, Billy. Kill me and your life is over.'

He laughed harshly. 'How many years do you think I've got left? Do you think they'll punish me more because I killed a cop?'

Jane shook her head. 'You're not killing a cop, Billy. Not tonight.' She threw the bottle at him with all her might. It span through the air and hit him in the face, knocking him backwards. He tumbled over a magazine rack and fell to the floor. He kept the knife in his hand and he roared with rage as he got to his feet.

Jane ran past him. He swung the knife at her and it snagged against her robe but didn't cut her. 'Bitch!' he shouted.

She reached the hallway, gasping for breath. The front door was double locked and the security chain was on and she knew she didn't have time to get it open before Billy would be at her back. There were two umbrellas in a rack by the door and she grabbed the largest, a red and white golfing umbrella with a polished wooden handle and a metal tip. As she turned, Billy came rushing out of the sitting room. He grinned when he saw the umbrella. 'Expecting rain?' he asked.

He raised the knife and stepped towards her. Jane lashed out with the umbrella and the metal tip caught him in the stomach. He swore as the tip stabbed into his flesh and drew blood. 'You fucking bitch!' he screamed. He took a step back and went into a crouch, moving the knife from side to side with his right hand as he clamped his left over his wound. She jabbed at him again, then clicked the bottom to open the umbrella and thrust it at him before turning to run upstairs.

Her bare feet thudded on the stairs and she heard Billy cursing in the hallway behind her, then a crashing sound as he stamped on the umbrella.

210

She reached the top of her stairs and took a quick look over her shoulder. Billy was coming after her, hatred in his eyes.

She got to her bedroom door, grabbed the handle and threw the door open,. She hurried inside, turned and slammed the door behind her. The brass key was in the lock and she turned it, then put her hands on either side of the door and stared at it, breathing heavily. The door was Victorian oak, as solid as a ship's timber, as were the jambs. It probably wouldn't stand up to a police-issued Enforcer battering ram, but she was fairly sure there was nothing an injured octogenarian could do to get through it, at least not before the police arrived.

She heard him pound up the stairs and then hesitate as he worked out which room she'd gone into. There were three bedrooms and a bathroom and all the other doors were open so he only paused for a second before stamping over to her bedroom. There was a long silence and Jane frowned as she listened, wondering what he would do. She turned her head to the side and pressed her ear against the wood, but all she could hear was the pounding of her own heart. She cursed under her breath as she realised she'd left her phone downstairs and there was no landline in the bedroom.

Something banged against the door so hard she felt the wood hit against her head and she jerked back, startled. Billy laughed as if he knew that he'd caught her by surprise. 'Come out, come out, wherever you are,' he said, and then cackled with laughter. 'Because if you don't, I'll huff and I'll puff and I'll blow this door down, little piggy.'

'Bastard,' muttered Jane under her breath. She pushed herself back and as she moved a scarf flashed over her face and before she could react it slipped under her chin against her throat and was pulled tight.

She tried to turn but whoever was behind her pushed her forward and her forehead hit the door. The scarf was pulled tighter and she made a gurgling sound as she tried in vain to get air into her lungs.

'Gotcha!' It was Charlie. She mentally cursed herself. Of course it was Charlie. Who the fuck else would it be?

'I've got her!' Charlie shouted at the top of his voice. 'I've fucking got her!'

Billy slammed his hand on the door. 'Let me in, I want a piece of her.'

Jane lifted her right leg and put her bare foot against the door, close to the handle. She grunted and pushed herself back as hard as she could. She banged into Charlie and he cursed and then the two of them fell backwards onto the bed. The towel around her hair came loose and fell to the floor.

Jane clawed at the scarf but she couldn't get her fingers underneath it. Her chest was heaving and burning and there was vomit at the back of her throat.

Jane tried to stand up but Charlie was too heavy and she fell back on to him. His legs were either side of her waist and she reached down and grabbed handfuls of his thighs and squeezed hard, digging her nails in. He screamed in pain and for a second he released his grip on the scarf and she managed to suck in half a lungful of air. He loosened her grip by kicking out with both legs and as she prepared to grab him again he rolled her over and off the bed. He fell on her heavily and she grunted in pain. As he pushed himself off her the scarf went loose and she took another breath.

'Bitch!' he shouted and yanked at the scarf.

Jane managed to get her hands in front of her and she put her palms face down and pushed hard. Charlie saw what she was doing and laughed. 'Yee ha, ride 'em cowboy!' he shouted, shifting his weight foward to push her back to the floor.

He pulled hard on the scarf and again Jane couldn't breathe. She put her fingers to her throat but there was no way she could get her fingers between the scarf and her skin.

Charlie started leaning back, adding his weight to the tension. Jane's eyes were bulging and her lungs felt as if they were on fire. She moved her hands again, pressed them against the floor, but this time pushed herself to the side, away from the bed. Charlie thought she was trying to get up so he moved forward and by the time he realised she was twisting to the side it was already too late and he was off balance. He kept hold of the scarf as he fell so Jane still couldn't breathe but once he was off her she rolled on top of him and elbowed him in the face. She caught him in the nose and he yelped. He pulled the scarf again but she was already moving, rolling off him and getting on to her hands and knees. He pulled hard and she jerked towards him, but then she went with the pressure and knelt on top of him. Her robe fell open

212

and her breasts swung free. Charlie's eyes flicked down and Jane took the opportunity to get her hands around his throat. She locked her thumbs on his trachea and dug her nails into the back of his neck.

His eyes widened and his upper lip curled back in a snarl. The scarf fell from his fingers and he reached up to grab her wrists. She glared at him in defiance as she tightened her grip on his throat. 'How do you like it, you bastard?' she hissed. He tried to pull her hands away but he was weak and she was strong, made stronger by the adrenaline coursing through her veins.

CHAPTER 41

'There!' shouted Archie, pointing at Jane's house. He cursed when he saw the Polo parked in the road. 'They're already here! Come on, come on!'

The patrol car screeched to a halt. PC Ahmed was out first and he ran full pelt past Jane's Lexus to the front door where he began ringing the doorbell. Archie jogged behind, pulling out a set of keys. 'It's okay, I've got keys.'

He fumbled through the keys until he found the right one, slotted it in and opened the door. It only opened a few inches before the security chain kicked in. Archie swore.

'Let me,' said PC Ahmed.

The constable hit the door with his shoulder twice, but when that didn't work he took a step back and kicked it, hard. The door flew open on the third kick. Archie pushed past him and went into the hallway. 'Jane!' he shouted.

PC Ahmed ran to the sitting room, then to the dining room as Archie headed up the stairs.

The driver appeared at the front door, calling in their location on her radio.

'Kitchen's clear!' shouted PC Ahmed.

Archie was halfway up the stairs when he saw Billy on the upstairs landing. He was holding a kitchen knife in his right hand. His left hand was bloody and clasped against his stomach,

Archie stopped and put his hands up. 'Billy, it's over,' he said,

'What the fuck? You're dead!'

'Obviously I'm not dead, mate.' He nodded at Billy's wound. 'What happened?'

214

'Your fucking daughter, that's what happened.' He laughed and then winced with pain. 'But Charlie is giving her what for.'

Archie took a step up but Billy waved his knife at him. 'I will fucking cut you, Archie.'

'No you won't, we're mates,' said Archie calmly.

'We're not fucking mates.'

Archie heard footsteps on the stairs behind him and PC Ahmed appeared at his shoulder. 'Step back please, sir,' he said to Archie.

'It's okay, I know Billy. He's not going to do anything stupid.'

PC Ahmed held out his hand to Billy. 'Give me the knife, Billy. No one needs to get hurt here.'

Billy laughed, took two quick steps forward and before PC Ahmed could react his hand was a bloody mess. The constable yelped, took a step back and lost his footing. He fell down the stairs, smearing blood on the wall.

'Billy, come on now, you're just going to make it worse,' said Archie.

'Fuck you,' said Billy.

Archie heard a popping sound and something whizzed by his left ear. Two prongs embedded themselves into Billy's chest and a fraction of a second later he slumped to the floor in spasm. Two fine wires led from the prongs to a bright yellow Taser in the hands of the patrol car driver. 'I love these things,' she said. 'You all right Ahmed?'

PC Ahmed was sitting with his back to the wall at the foot of the stairs, nursing his injured hand.

'I'm okay.'

'Rule number one of negotiating with a knife-wielding nutter?'

'Don't stick your hand out.'

'Exactly,' she said.

Archie stepped over Billy, who had stopped trembling and was now lying still. He grabbed the handle of the door and twisted it, but the door was locked. He banged his hand on it. 'Jane!' He hit the door again. 'Jane, are you okay?'

'Step away from the door, sir,' said the woman. Her taser had two shots and she had it aimed at the door, her finger on the trigger.

The handle clicked and turned and the door opened. It was Jane. She was wearing a white bath robe and her hair was unkempt and her face was bathed in sweat. She looked at Archie, smiled with relief, and collapsed into his arms.

The driver moved quickly, her taser at the ready. Charlie was lying on his back by the bed, his eyes closed and his mouth open.

'Is he...?' asked Archie.

Jane shook her head. 'He's not dead, dad. He passed out, that's all.'

'You're okay?'

She forced a smile. 'I'm okay, but I've had better days.'

He hugged her and rested his chin on her head.

'What took you so long to get here?' she asked.

'The traffic was terrible.'

CHAPTER 42

By time they were ready to bring Charlie down and put him in the back of the police van, Jane had put on a grey suit and tied back her hair. Within minutes of her coming out of the bedroom, a second police car had arrived and not long after that an ambulance had turned up, blue lights flashing. Paramedics had stabilised Billy's stomach wound and slapped a temporary dressing on PC Ahmed's cut hand, and given Charlie the all-clear. Other than bruises around his neck, Charlie was unhurt and he sat on the bed with his hands cuffed behind his back until a van arrived to transport him to the Marton HQ for processing. The ambulance took Billy and Ahmed to the Royal Preston Hospital, without the flashing lights. Billy was handcuffed to his gurney and there was a PC with him.

Archie and Jane were standing by the van when they brought Charlie down. He was escorted by two burly uniformed constables who were holding an elbow each. He sneered when he saw Archie. 'How are you not dead?'

'Just lucky, I guess.'

Charlie shook his head. 'I must have lost my touch.'

'You're old,' said Jane. 'But at least all your victims will finally get some sort of justice.'

Charlie took a deep breath and sighed. 'You know what's funny?' he asked Archie.

'Funny ha-ha or funny peculiar?'

'Funny funny. You're sending me to prison and you know what?'

'What?'

Charlie grinned savagely. 'I'll be better off than where I was. TV in my room, choice of meals, and free health care and dental. You know how many prisoners died in jail during the coronavirus

217

outbreak? A few dozen. You know how many old folk died in so-called care homes? Twenty thousand plus. They threw the old folk under a bus but bent over backwards to protect the prisoners. We're better off in prison, Archie. Think about that when you're in a care home for real, eating shit food and being abused by so-called carers who hate your guts.'

Jane slipped her arm around Archie. 'You couldn't be more wrong,' she said. 'Dad won't ever be in a nursing home, because he'll have me to take care of him. That's the difference between you and my dad. Dad's got someone who loves him.'

Charlie scowled at her but before he could say anything, the PCs pushed him into the back of the van and slammed the door shut.

'That was a nice thing to say,' said Archie, as the van drove away.

'I meant it, dad.'

'Thanks, love.'

'Do you want to come to HQ with me? I want to be the one to formally charge them and I think you should be there when it happens.'

Archie grinned. 'I'd be honoured.' He hugged her and kissed her on the top of her head. 'I did potty train you, you know.'

Jane shook her head and laughed. 'No, you didn't.'